LEVI

HELL SQUAD #15

ANNA HACKETT

Levi

Published by Anna Hackett

Copyright 2018 by Anna Hackett

Cover by Melody Simmons of eBookindiecovers

Edits by Tanya Saari

ISBN (ebook): 978-1-925539-41-7

ISBN (paperback): 978-1-925539-42-4

Unexplored – Romantic Book of the Year (Ruby) Novella Winner 2017

At Star's End – One of Library Journal's Best E-Original Romances for 2014

Return to Dark Earth – One of Library Journal's Best E-Original Books for 2015 and two-time SFR Galaxy Awards winner

The Phoenix Adventures – SFR Galaxy Award Winner for Most Fun New Series and "Why Isn't This a Movie?" Series

Beneath a Trojan Moon – SFR Galaxy Award Winner and RWAus Ella Award Winner

Hell Squad – Amazon Bestselling Science Fiction Romance Series and SFR Galaxy Award for best Post-Apocalypse for Readers who don't like Post-Apocalypse

The Anomaly Series – #1 Amazon Action Adventure Romance Bestseller

"Like Indiana Jones meets Star Wars. A treasure hunt with a steamy romance." – SFF Dragon, review of *Among Galactic Ruins*

"Strap in, enjoy the heat of romance and the daring of this group of space travellers!" – Di, Top 500 Amazon Reviewer, review of *At Star's End*

"Action, danger, aliens, romance – yup, it's another great book from Anna Hackett!" – Book Gannet Reviews, review of *Hell Squad: Marcus*

Sign up for my VIP mailing list and get your *free box set* containing three action-packed romances.

Visit here to get started:
www.annahackettbooks.com

CHAPTER ONE

L evi King slammed his foot down on the accelerator and spun the wheel.

The heavily armored Z6-Hunter responded, skidding left. Levi narrowly avoided the oncoming alien vehicle by a few centimeters. He gunned the Hunter across the bumpy, deteriorating road.

He grinned.

"Hold this fucking thing still," a deep voice yelled from the back of the vehicle.

Levi knew when his best mate, Ash Connors, was angry. And right now, he was pissed. The man was currently manning the autocannon at the back of the Hunter, trying to take down the aliens.

Turning the vehicle again, and holding it as damn still as he could, Levi watched green laser fire trace through the air. He turned the wheel again and spotted a raptor vehicle straight ahead. He clenched his teeth.

About the same size as the Hunter, it was a black, squat-looking thing with solid plating, four rugged tires, and three sharp spikes in front that made it look like a triceratops. That made Levi and his squad mates call them trikes.

The trike let out a blast of alien weapons fire—a dark-green poison that could burn through just about anything. He jerked the Hunter to the side. Their own laser fire struck the alien vehicle, and it spun out of control before crashing into a tree.

Levi grinned. *Yeah, baby*.

"Woo-hoo!" Beside Levi, Hemi—their squad's second-in-command—shouted and barked out a laugh. The bearded man had his carbine aimed out the side window. "Take that, you alien assholes."

Another black trike came into view, and Levi jerked the wheel again. He swung the Hunter around, getting into position so Ash would have a clear shot on the cannon.

Across the clash of fighting, he saw another Hunter zooming fast toward them, across the overgrown grass of a nearby field. That one had the rest of his squad mates in it—their squad leader Tane, ex-con and former cop, Griff, and dark, scary Dom.

They were Squad Three, also known as the berserkers, fighting to protect their little outpost of humanity from the invading Gizzida aliens.

The afternoon's routine patrol had turned deadly when they'd run into this group of alien vehicles. Fuckers had appeared out of nowhere, and they'd had almost no advance warning.

Levi's hands tightened on the wheel. He didn't care. He liked taking down raptors.

"Bring us around again," Ash yelled.

"On it." Levi pushed more speed out of the Hunter. They didn't often get to take these vehicles out, preferring their armored bikes, so he was enjoying the hell out of it. You had to find some fucking fun where you could.

Some days, it felt like he'd been fighting his entire life —as a boy, raised by a rough biker dad, he'd grown up dodging fists and learning how to use his own. As an outspoken teen, fighting for his place in the world. And finally, as the president of a motorcycle club he'd been forced to drag out of the blood and filth of the wrong side of the law. And now, as a berserker, fighting back against the dinosaur-like invading aliens.

Levi had been born into rough and he was still living rough.

"What the fuck is that?" Hemi's deep voice rumbled through the vehicle.

Levi turned his head and saw a giant alien vehicle coming out of the haze of laser fire.

Fucking hell. It was at least twice the size of the other alien trike vehicles, with eight wheels under it, and a giant row of armor plates down the back of it. Damn thing looked like a stegosaurus.

"Squad Three, you have a large alien vehicle incoming." A female voice came through the comms on the central console. "I'm reading thicker armor plating than the trikes, and more weapons."

Indy Bennett was their outspoken comms officer, sitting back at the Enclave. She was a wildcat who wasn't afraid of the bikers, mercs, and criminals who made up their squad.

Levi wasn't worried about the size of the steg. He was more concerned about the giant, spinning saw blades on the front of it.

"Ash," Levi called out.

"I see it," Ash answered. "Bring us around."

"Levi? Hemi?" This time, a deep, controlled voice came through the comm unit. It was Tane—Squad Three's leader and Hemi's brother.

"We're on it, Tane," Levi answered.

He sped up, turning the Hunter in a wide circle around the steg. Through the long window at the front of the alien vehicle, just behind the giant saw, he caught a quick glimpse of several raptors sitting at the controls inside.

Ugly-ass creatures. The raptors were humanoid, with thick, gray, hairless skin, and teeth. A hell of a lot of teeth. And nobody could forget the glowing red eyes.

Ash fired the autocannon. Laser blasts hit the side of the steg, but didn't seem to have much impact. The vehicle turned around, moving pretty damn fast for such a massive thing.

Fuck. Levi threw all his focus into driving. He spun the Hunter's wheel and jammed his foot down on the accelerator. As the steg roared toward them, he swung the Hunter into some fancy maneuvers.

The entire time, Ash kept shooting, the cannon whining. Across the field, Levi saw the other Hunter circling the steg and firing as well. The top hatch of the second

Hunter was open and Tane's dread-locked head was visible as he fired his carbine.

"It's coming around again," Hemi shouted.

Levi turned the Hunter, driving off the cracked road and onto the grass. He felt a hard thump at the front end of the Hunter and he righted them. *Damn.* Must have hit something in the grass. Then he got into position, directly facing the steg.

Suddenly, the Hunter's engine faltered.

Fuck. No, dammit. He jammed his foot on the accelerator. Nothing.

The engine died.

"Levi!" Ash shouted.

"I'm working on it!" Levi tried to stay calm, his heart trying to knock its way out of his damn chest. He tried to start the engine, but there was no response. He looked up...and saw the steg bearing down on them, the giant saw blade spinning faster and faster.

Shit. He worked the controls. "Come on, baby, don't do this to us."

The steg roared closer.

The Hunter's engine caught, then died again. *Come on, come on.* Levi punched buttons and pushed gears, trying to get the vehicle started.

"Levi, this fucking century," Hemi growled.

"Something's fucking wrong with the engine."

"I knew I should have driven," Ash muttered.

"Fuck you, Connors."

The steg got closer, looming over them, the blades a gleaming, metallic blur.

The Hunter's engine roared to life, with a belching growl. Levi jerked the wheel.

The saw blades sliced into the Hunter's right side. The vehicle jolted, sparks flying, and there was the vicious screech of metal being ripped open. Ash was firing from the turret and shouting. Levi jerked the gears. They needed to back up. Hemi leaped into the back seat, the crazy man firing through the tear in the Hunter, directly at the saw.

Levi slammed his boot on the accelerator and reversed the vehicle, turning the wheel.

With a huge jolt that rocked the Hunter, and another shriek of metal on metal, they tore free of the saw blades.

Levi reversed them back until Ash was in perfect firing range. Laser fire lit up the afternoon sky, and a second later, Tane's Hunter roared up beside them. Together, the autocannons on the two Hunters fired on the steg.

Sparks poured out of a damaged side panel on the giant alien vehicle. A moment later, under the unrelenting hail of laser fire, it pulled back and fled.

Levi pulled the Hunter to a stop and dropped his head to the wheel. "Fuck."

"What the hell happened?" Ash called out.

"We lost all power. The engine stopped." At the worst possible time.

The Hunters, and the other gear the squads used in combat, were taken care of by dedicated maintenance teams. With most of the world around them destroyed, it wasn't like they could order a new vehicle or quadcopter.

And the lead Hunter mechanic was a luscious redhead with killer curves and a sharp tongue. Well, Levi had a few things to say to her.

Hemi leaned in from the back seat and slapped him on the back. "I'll buy you a beer when we get back to the Enclave."

"Fuck," Levi said. "I'm gonna need more than one."

CHRISSY HAGAN STOOD in the Hunter maintenance bay, waiting. She hitched up her toolbelt and stared impatiently at the large doors at the end of the cavernous space. She'd heard from the comms team that one of her Hunters had been damaged on the latest mission.

She tapped the toe of her boot on the stained concrete. The Hunters were her babies. Since she'd arrived at the Enclave, an underground human sanctuary south of the ruins of Sydney, working on the Hunters had given her purpose in the chaos.

God, some days she still woke, thinking she was back in her apartment in Miami, and about to head to the garage where she'd worked with her father.

Reality was that her once-in-a-lifetime vacation to Australia had turned into an alien invasion and fight for survival. Horrible memories stirred and she shoved them away.

Instead, she looked over at the parked Hunter beside her. She ran a hand over the dark armor plating. Every vehicle, Hunter, quadcopter, and piece of tech they had was precious. There were no more factories, from which they could get new parts, or new vehicles. They had to scrape together what they needed to keep these babies going...their survival depended on it.

Thankfully, fixing engines was in Chrissy's blood. She'd inherited that particular skill from her dad.

The Hagan Auto Shop had been small, but known for quality work. She'd loved going to work every day, even working with her big, burly, and sometimes down-right difficult father. Pain clenched in her chest. A while ago, she'd managed to get confirmation from a human base hidden in the Everglades that the part of Miami where the garage had been located had been completely decimated.

Her father was gone.

She'd always known Stan Hagan wanted sons. Chrissy barely remembered her mom, who'd died when Chrissy was a small girl, not long after Chrissy's sister, Jussy, had been born. Instead, her father had ended up alone, raising two small girls. He'd done his best.

Sadness pierced her. He'd driven her crazy, but she also missed him. Chrissy stroked the Hunter again. She had no idea if Jussy had made it. Her sister had run off with her six-month-old daughter just before the invasion. Chrissy rubbed her chest. She'd tried to do everything she could to make her dad happy, but Jussy had been the wild child who never did anything right.

Chrissy blew out a breath, wondering if Jussy and her tiny niece, Charlee, were holed up somewhere safe. *Hope you made it, J-girl.*

The hangar bay doors rumbled open, and the deep growl of the Hunter engines echoed in the space. She straightened.

All the squads were rough on the vehicles, but she knew exactly which squad had the Hunters today. She wrinkled her nose. Squad Three, aka the berserkers. That group of wild ones were the hardest on the equipment.

Scary Tane mostly kept his team in line. The man was sexy as hell, but most women were afraid of him. Chrissy had one word to sum up each of the berserkers. After Scary Tane, there was Wild Hemi, Handsome Ash, Intense Dom, Hard Griff and Cocky Levi.

They sure were a motley bunch of bearded and tattooed bad boys.

One was the baddest of all.

Nope. She wasn't going to think of him. Or the fact that a few weeks back, they'd sniped at each other in a corridor...and she'd ended up grabbing his crotch. And a very hard, very large... She groaned. Nope, a hundred times. *Definitely* not thinking about that. Hopefully she could avoid talking to him, as well. Because every time Levi King opened his mouth, she wanted to whack him in the teeth with her wrench.

The first Hunter rolled in. Her tense muscles relaxed. Apart from a few new scratches and a singed section thanks to raptor poison, it didn't look too bad.

Then she saw the second Hunter. Her gut clenched and she hissed out a breath. *No.*

She stared in horror at the tear down the side of the vehicle. It looked like it had been ripped open by a can opener.

The vehicles pulled to a stop and she kept staring at the damaged Hunter. The driver's door opened and a man-bunned, tattooed menace got out. He was clad in black armor, except for his arms, allowing him to display some of his tattoos.

Horror morphed to anger. "What the hell did you do to my Hunter, biker man?" She stomped toward him.

Levi's head whipped around and he grinned at her. "Hey there, Spitfire. I didn't do it, the Gizzida did."

Chrissy resisted the urge to punch him in the gut.

"Tane didn't get his Hunter sliced open like a tin can." She flung out an arm. "Clearly, you suck at driving."

Levi's whiskey-brown eyes narrowed. "I'm a fucking excellent driver. I'm better at it than you are at maintaining these things." He kicked the Hunter's tire.

She sucked in her breath. "How dare you—?"

"Damn thing stalled, right as a giant-ass alien vehicle with a saw attached to the front of it was bearing down on us." He crossed his arms over his chest. "Not my happiest moment. Ash and Hemi were pretty unhappy too."

Her eyes widened, and she spared a brief glance for Ash and Hemi. Both men were leaning against the Hunter, watching them, and grinning.

She scowled back at Levi. "What?"

"It stopped. Engine cut out." He stroked his trim—and damn him, sexy—goatee. "No power. Nothing."

Chrissy pressed one hand to her hip and frowned. "It was in perfect condition when you took it out." Brushing past him, she reached over and opened the hood.

"I'm going to debrief with the general," Tane called out. "Good work out there. Get some down time."

She barely listened to the hum of deep murmurs as the other berserkers replied. Bootsteps thudded on the concrete around her as they left.

She hoped Levi would go with them, but as she leaned in to look at the Hunter engine, she felt a big, hard body press in close behind her.

Annoyed, she jammed her elbow back. The asshole was still wearing his armor, so she knew he wouldn't have felt anything.

"Out of my way, biker man." She spotted some damage at the back of the engine and frowned. It looked almost melted. "How the hell did you get it damaged in here? Do you give a shit about anything—?"

Suddenly, fingers hooked in the back of her tool belt and yanked her backward. Chrissy spun around to face a very annoyed-looking biker.

"You don't know me," he growled.

"I know your type."

He grinned. *God.* She hated that even his damn grin was sexy.

"You don't know anyone like me, Spitfire."

He was right, the cocky bastard, but Chrissy was never going to admit that. Ever. "Keep dreaming, biker man. I've seen my share of cocky, tattooed bikers. They were either hitting on me, or talking down to the *dumb widdle* female mechanic." She lifted her chin. "You've done both."

Levi leaned closer, and she got a whiff of man and healthy, male sweat.

"I've seen the work you do on the Hunters, Spitfire. I've rebuilt more car and bike engines than I can count, and I'm not doubting your skills. You work magic with them."

She blinked. Her father had been grudging as hell with praise. Now, just a few words from a man who annoyed the hell out of her made her warm inside.

Get a grip, Chrissy.

"But I'm also not blind," Levi continued. "You have a fantastic ass, and the way your T-shirts hug your—"

Chrissy slammed a hand to his chest. "I get it. God, you were almost nice there, but you just had to add some asshole to it, didn't you?"

He shrugged, grin in place. "Just telling you how it is." Then his face turned serious. "The Hunter did stop at a crucial fucking moment, Chrissy."

She nodded, glancing back at the damage in the engine. "I'll find out why." She made a shooing motion with her hand. "Now go. I've got work to do."

He stared at her a long moment. She was pretty sure Levi King didn't take orders unless he wanted to.

"Am I too distracting?"

She rolled her eyes. "Just go."

When he turned to leave, she huffed out a breath. *Annoying man.* It was really so wrong that such an annoying man could smell so good, especially after a mission.

Shoving Levi King and his man bun out of her head, she kicked her iono-creeper over. She dropped onto it and laid flat, then pushed herself in under the Hunter. The creeper used electrohydrodynamics to hover a few inches off the ground.

She looked up at the melted mass of metal above her.

Time to get to work.

CHAPTER TWO

L evi took a long sip of his homebrew beer and dropped back into a chair.

The rec room was humming tonight, with Enclave residents out for a drink, some cards, or a game of pool.

"Damn, that's good." A beer and a soft chair. He'd take his pleasure where he could after a tough mission.

Ash sat down beside him, pulling his woman into his lap. Pretty, geeky Marin smiled, her cheeks a little pink as she pushed her blonde curls out of her face. Glasses were perched on the end of a cute nose.

Levi grinned. His friend was completely whipped, and Levi was happy for him. Like Levi, Ash had grown up rough, and life had thrown plenty of shit at him. He was a good man—the best. Ash deserved a pretty geek girl who made him happy.

Not that Levi wanted the same thing. Love and beauty...it didn't hang around him for long. Hell, his dad hadn't set a great example. Damien King's idea of family was slapping his kid in the face when it suited him. *You are good for nothing, boy. I've got better things to do.* Levi's hands tightened.

His bitch of an ex-wife hadn't loved him, either—Tiff had loved his cock and his bank account.

Nope, love and beauty were not for Levi King. He'd accepted that a long time ago.

Tane, showered and dreadlocks tied at the back of his neck, leaned against a nearby high, round table. Griff and Dom were with him. They were talking about the steg and its capabilities. Levi knew Tane had briefed the general on the new alien vehicle.

"Where's my beer?" Hemi's voice boomed behind Levi.

Levi looked over his shoulder and saw Hemi with his arm around his woman. Cam was a long, tall drink of gorgeous, dark-skinned woman.

Tane pushed a bottle across the table. "Cam, need anything?"

"No thanks, Tane." There was a faint Scottish burr to her voice.

Hemi grinned. "I just gave her everything she needed." He moved his hand behind Cam.

Cam gripped his thick wrist, her eyes narrowed. "If you slap my ass, Rahia, we are going to have big problems."

"But it's such a fine ass."

The Squad Nine soldier shook her head, cupped Hemi's bearded cheeks, and yanked him in for a hard kiss. "I'm due to meet Mac, Taylor, and Sienna...try to stay out of trouble."

"Never." Hemi winked at her.

With a sigh, Cam left with a wave.

Levi leaned back, listening to his friends shoot the shit.

"Hey, Levi." A pretty blonde named Jennifer appeared, shooting him a friendly smile. "Thought you might want some company."

Usually, after a mission, Levi was more than up for company of the female kind. He lifted his drink, his gaze moving past her. "Not tonight, sweetheart."

Jennifer's mouth opened, then with a shrug, she headed off.

"You sick?" Ash asked, eyeing him. "Coming down with something."

"No."

"You never blow off a woman."

"Drop it, Ash." But Levi recognized that look in his best friend's eyes.

"And there sure are plenty of them interested in bedding a sexy, bad boy berserker," a feminine voice drawled.

Indy stood with one hip cocked. The tattooed, out-spoken woman did and said what she wanted, when she wanted it. She was the only comms officer who'd been able to keep up with the berserkers. She was also a family friend of Griff's. The man had been best mates with Indy's brother, and he still felt the need to look out for her...which she didn't much appreciate. Right now, Griff was glaring at Indy's back.

With a laugh, she sat on Levi's lap. "Don't worry, Levi, I'll run decoy and protect you."

He smiled, easing an arm around her. Indy was attractive, but she was like a sister to him...if he'd had a sister.

"I'm out of here." Griff set his half-finished beer down.

Indy arched a brow. "Oh? Hot date?"

Levi didn't do subtle, but even he was picking up the vibes. He glanced at Ash, who arched a brow.

"Going to catch up with Manu at the firing range." Griff shoved his hands in his pockets. "See you later."

The oldest Rahia brother was a former berserker. Toughest guy Levi knew. Manu could fire any weapon and charge into a fight without a single flicker of fear. Levi swirled his beer. Manu had lost his leg on a mission that had gone to fucking hell and it had put him off active duty. But he managed to rule the firing range with an iron fist.

Looking up, Levi spotted a flash of auburn hair and straightened. Chrissy strode across the room, heading for the self-service bar. She had bulky gray coveralls on, but had the top of them down and the sleeves tied around her waist. Her tight white tank made him slide his tongue across his teeth.

She smiled at someone and he saw a streak of grease on her cheek.

Fuck. When had the sight of grease on a woman's skin turned him on? He watched her grab some cans of soda from the fridges, then head back toward the door, winding around some chairs and tables.

Her head lifted and their gazes caught. Her blue eyes narrowed before they flicked to Indy nestled in his lap.

Damn, he wanted her. And he couldn't wait much longer. She might want to ignore the pull, but he didn't.

"Hey, Chrissy," Ash called out. "You guys still working on the Hunters?"

She paused, her arms full of cans, and nodded. "Yep. Cleaning up after you guys."

There were deep laughs.

"How's the damaged Hunter?" Tane asked.

"Damaged. I already have our armor plating guy fixing the outer panels, but the damage to the engine is extensive." She glared at Levi. "You could take a little more care, King."

Indy snorted and Levi pushed her off his lap. "You could make sure the damn thing doesn't stop in the middle of a firefight."

Chrissy tossed her head back, red hair sliding over her shoulders. "I downloaded the engine stats. You rev it too much and you're hell on the steering—"

"Fighting aliens, babe. It isn't a Sunday drive."

He heard snorts and poorly smothered laughter from the guys.

She ground her teeth together. "You still don't need—"

He stepped closer to her. "It's dangerous out there."

She took a step closer, her eyes full of fire. "I know that. I was locked in an alien prison, remember?"

His boots bumped hers. "If we're ever going to beat them, we need reliable gear or we're dead."

"Then have more respect for it," she hissed. "You somehow melted the engine. It looks like a hot poker was shoved through it—"

"Then you need more protective plating."

She drew up. "I don't tell you how to lob a grenade, so don't tell me how to do my job, biker man. I don't care if you were king mechanic of a badass biker garage before the invasion."

Damn, she was something. Her cheeks were flushed, her blue eyes spitting fire, and that mouth...she always had something to say. He grinned.

An annoyed, aggravated sound came from her throat. She lifted her arm and threw a drink can at him.

Levi caught it an inch from his face. His squad mates broke out in guffaws.

"That wasn't nice."

"I'm not nice," she snapped.

He leaned closer and lowered his voice. "Neither am I."

She pulled in a deep breath, then spun and strode out.

"Damn," Hemi said. "You two should sell tickets."

Indy fanned her face. "I'm heading back to my room for some *alone time*."

"Shit." Levi shook his head. "I need another beer."

"PASS ME THE WRENCH," Chrissy said, holding out her hand.

The tool was set gently in her palm. She glanced over at her offsider and smiled.

Max grinned back. He was a sturdy boy of five with a mop of dark hair. She'd helped rescue him from the

Gizzida and they'd been firm friends ever since. He lived with a lovely foster family here in the Enclave, but she hung out with him whenever she could.

She leaned back into the Hunter engine, working to loosen some of the melted parts. She was pretty sure there was more damage in here that she couldn't see.

Chrissy pulled off a melted bit of metal and the memory of her showdown with Levi in the rec room reverberated through her head. The man managed to light the fuse on her temper faster than anyone she knew.

Shaking her head, she handed the ruined part to Max. "Set it over there for me. With the pile of other damaged parts." Max happily complied.

He loved sitting with her while she worked and over the weeks, it had been so good to see his solemn face start to relax and his smile start to blossom.

She tugged off more parts, listening to Max talk about his schoolwork. He loved math, and tolerated reading and writing. Art and music were fun, and playing sports was his favorite thing.

A hammer banged on metal nearby. She couldn't see him, but she knew her fellow maintenance team member, John, was working on the torn side plating. The tall, thin man was a genius at that sort of work. It wouldn't be beautiful afterward, but it would be functional, and that was all that mattered.

"Max?"

They both looked up. Max's foster father, Jonas, was standing at the bay doors, smiling.

"We need to get home for dinner, Maxie," the man said.

Max hopped off his perch beside her toolbox. "Bye, Chrissy."

She held her arms out. "I'm a bit grimy..."

He wrapped his arms around her. "I don't mind."

She held him tight and breathed him in. This is what they were fighting for. Chrissy vowed that she would do anything to keep this boy safe and give him a fighting chance. He'd suffered enough.

Watching him take his foster father's hand and skip out left a smile on her face. She went back to work on her engine.

Another hour slipped by, and the Hunter hangar slowly emptied of workers as they headed back to their quarters.

"How's it going in there?"

Chrissy straightened, pressing her hands to her lower back to ease the aching muscles. Another maintenance mechanic, Rebecca, stood beside her. This week, Bec's shoulder length hair was colored pale pink, framing her round face. She changed it every week. Chrissy had asked her about it, and Bec had told her that before the invasion she'd always wanted to dye her hair, but hadn't because her work would have frowned on one of their engineers with blue or pink or green hair. Since the invasion, the young woman had vowed to dye her hair every week with her own homemade dyes.

"Progress?" Bec asked.

"Slow progress. Whatever happened, it burned everything in the back of the engine to shit."

"What can I do to help?"

Chrissy picked up her portable comp and tapped the

screen. "I've made a list of the replacement parts I need. Can you print them out for me?"

Bec manned the 3D printer they used to manufacture small parts. She eyed the screen.

"Sure thing. Shoot the list through to me and I'll get to work." Her nose wrinkled. "Hopefully I've got all the metal we'll need for them."

"Running low?"

"Always." She tucked some pink hair back behind her ear, her gaze on the engine. "Hey, I saw you updated the rotor and changed out the insulation. The changes were genius."

Chrissy grinned. "Thanks. I like to tinker in my spare time."

Bec rolled her eyes. "You should be having fun in your spare time."

"Heard you were having fun with Eric from the tech team."

A wide grin. "He's shy and gets tongue tied around me. It's so cute. I'm meeting him for dinner. Don't work too late." The woman headed off with a wave.

Chrissy went back to work. She had no one to meet for dinner and she wanted to get this Hunter operational.

She'd pulled off most of the damaged parts. She pulled her scanning device off her belt and flicked it on. It made a few beeps, info filling the small screen. Then she heard it emit a loud, long beep. She frowned. There was an abnormal power spike. She leaned in farther to get a closer look.

All of a sudden, something small, black, and slimy leaped out of the engine compartment at her.

What the hell?

Chrissy threw her hands up in a defensive motion, and felt slimy tentacles snake along her scanner and wrist. The thing looked like a small, black octopus. Its gelatinous head turned and two red eyes stared balefully at her.

Alien eyes.

Suddenly, the thing moved, aiming for her face.

CHAPTER THREE

S tumbling back, Chrissy desperately tried to keep the alien creature away from her face.

Two slimy, black tentacles waved in front of her eyes, then wrapped around her wrist. Hard. She dropped the scanner and it clattered on the floor.

She spun around. "You little fucker, you're what damaged my Hunter." She steeled herself, and with her other hand, she gripped the slick creature, trying to pull the alien off her.

The tentacles around her wrist tightened. *Ow*. They continued to tighten and pain flared up her arm.

Chrissy stumbled again and cried out. The next instant, she heard a bone snap and electric pain burned up her arm.

"What the fuck?" Suddenly, strong, tattooed arms wrapped around her from behind. Levi gripped the alien, adding his strength to hers.

But the alien wouldn't budge. It jostled her broken wrist and nausea washed through her from the pain.

Levi grunted. "Hit it."

Trusting him to hold it from moving, she let go with her other hand. She yanked a hammer off her belt and aimed for the creature. She hit it and she felt the tentacles tighten more. The strike reverberated through her wrist and she screamed.

"Hold on, Spitfire."

Levi shuffled them across the hangar, and with each step, the pain worsened. Her vision wavering, she saw he was moving them toward her toolbox.

"Chrissy, stay with me, honey. Grab something out of there and slice that fucker up."

Fighting to stay conscious, she reached out and grabbed a laser cutter out of the toolbox. She flicked it on and orange light flared. She thrust the cutter at the alien, careful to avoid Levi's hands.

The creature's tentacles went wild, and she watched the alien change color from black to mottled red, and back again. She stabbed it once more.

It released its hold on her and dropped to the ground, curling in on itself. Sweet relief filled her, and she slumped against Levi's body.

"You're all right, Spitfire." He held her close to his chest.

She glanced back at the alien. The damned thing was slowly trying to drag its injured body under a Hunter. "It's not dead! We have to stop it."

She shuddered at the thought of that thing getting into the Enclave. There were kids out there, like Max. A boy who'd already suffered too much. This thing was added fuel to the nightmares.

Levi scowled and snatched a wrench off her belt. As he moved toward the alien, it changed directions, heading for some storage crates. It slithered under them.

Swallowing down her pain, Chrissy grabbed the laser cutter and followed. She clutched her injured hand to her chest.

"You shift the crates," she said.

He eyed her and nodded. "Ready?"

She met his gaze and lifted the laser cutter. "Ready."

He slammed a boot into the crate, tipping it over.

The alien was ready, flying up at them.

Chrissy dodged to the side. The animal landed, splayed on the floor, and pushed up on its tentacles to turn back.

Levi lifted a boot and brought it down on one tentacle, pinning it. "Now!"

She raced forward with the laser cutter. The creature whipped around in a frenzy. She hesitated for a second, worried that she'd hit Levi.

"Do it!" he ordered.

She thrust the cutter into the creature.

Tentacles waved wildly and it flickered black and red.

Levi lifted his boot and slammed it down on the creature. The flailing tentacles stopped and flopped to the concrete.

He stepped back and sucked in a deep breath. "What the fuck was that?"

Chrissy clutched her broken wrist to her chest, and

on a hunch, went over to get her scanner. She wasn't sure this would work, but she flicked the device on and scanned the creature.

Data appeared on the screen and she hissed. "Well, it isn't just an ugly Gizzida pet, after all. It's part animal and part machine. This is what disabled the Hunter." She frowned. "It looks like there's data stored on this thing." She looked up at Levi. "It was designed to collect data."

He frowned. "Shit. Come on. We need to let the geek squad know, and get your arm checked out."

Chrissy nodded. She knew that Noah Kim and his team of geniuses who kept everything in the Enclave running were the best people to pull this little nasty apart.

Besides, she really wanted a painkiller.

"The little bastard broke my wrist," she muttered.

"Broke it?" Levi reached out, gently touching her arm. He muttered a savage curse, then grabbed the back of his T-shirt and yanked it over his head.

She watched, mesmerized.

"Here." He set to work fashioning a makeshift sling for her.

Chrissy was too busy staring at his chest, and the vast expanse of bronzed skin over hard, lean muscle. She swallowed. Silver winked at her from one of his flat nipples. God, he had a nipple ring. And all that black ink. Her gaze followed some tribal markings that ran down his side.

Then he turned and she got a view of his back.

Oh. God. Chrissy had always liked tattoos on a man.

Levi's muscled back was completely covered in the most amazing ink. She shifted, her gaze sliding over the outstretched black wings of a fallen warrior angel.

He turned back. "Come on, we need to get you to the infirmary."

Infirmary. *Right*. Broken wrist.

He slid an arm around her and scooped her into his arms.

She gasped. "My arm's broken, King, not my legs."

"Don't care." He strode out of the hangar.

"What about the alien?"

"I'll call Noah from the infirmary." Levi paused. "You did good work back there, Spitfire. Didn't lose your cool once."

Praise from this man shouldn't feel so good. "Thanks. You too."

He'd charged in with no concern for his own safety. She'd heard the berserkers were good at that.

Suddenly, he grinned at her. "Wow, you thanked me without spontaneously combusting."

She screwed her nose up. "Don't ruin it."

He leaned closer, his breath brushing her cheek. "I can't wait for you to thank me for giving you the best orgasm of your life."

"Annnnd he's ruined it. You just can't help but be an asshole, can you?"

He turned a corner into another corridor and ahead lay the door into the infirmary. "Nope. Come on, Spitfire. Let's get that arm fixed."

"And then I can punch you with it," she grumbled.

LEVI LEANED against the wall in the Command Center, staring at the small crowd gathered for the early-morning briefing. Ash and Tane were flanking him.

His gaze moved unerringly to auburn hair sitting close to the front. Chrissy had tossed him some glares when he'd forced her to sit. Her wrist was all healed now, but it would take him a while to forget the sight of her wrestling with that alien thing when he'd entered the hangar.

"All right, let's get started." General Holmes stepped out in front. The man carried an air of authority that usually grated on Levi, but Holmes did get the job done. He made tough choices, took action, and kept everyone in this little sanctuary of humanity alive.

Off to the side stood another dark-haired man. Niko Ivanov was the civilian leader of the Enclave. The man was an artist, but Levi recognized a badass when he saw one. He might be an artist now, but he'd been *something else* before. From the day the survivors from Blue Mountain Base had arrived, Niko had welcomed them and worked seamlessly with Holmes to make the Enclave their home too.

"Noah's had some time to study the creature that came off the Hunter."

Noah stood, his dark hair loose and brushing his shoulders, and a frown on his face. He held a device and when he clicked a button, images blinked onto the screens covering the wall. They all showed the ugly, black tentacle creature.

"We're calling this unattractive little guy a parasite. It is an organic machine, and seems to have been specifically designed to get into the Hunter, lay low, and collect data."

Levi glanced at Chrissy and caught her wince. Hell, the woman even looked sexy when she was uncomfortable. He took in her black tank top, and the way it showcased slender arms and her fantastic breasts. His cock hardened and he let himself imagine her naked.

She didn't look his way, and he got the distinct impression she was ignoring him.

Levi had learned to never give up. If you wanted something, you went after it, because life was a bitch. She never handed you anything for free. You fought for it, and you bled for it, or you got nothing.

God, Chrissy had been fierce fighting that creature. No screaming or hysterics. Tough as fuck, even with a broken wrist.

"What data is this thing collecting?" Marcus Steel, the leader of Hell Squad, asked.

"Everything," Noah answered. "How the Hunter works, info about the fuel systems, engine stats, and weapons data."

"The maintenance team is already checking all our vehicles and Hawks for any sign of more of these things," Holmes said. "I've also got extra squads out on patrol." He glanced at the woman standing tall beside him.

Captain Kate Scott, head of Enclave security, nodded. "My security team is on high alert. If anyone gets close to the Enclave, we'll know about it."

"I did get some encrypted alien data off the parasite." A satisfied smile crossed Noah's face. "Elle?"

A small brunette seated at a comp tapped on the screen. Elle Steele, comms officer for Hell Squad and Marcus' wife, smiled as she worked.

Images flashed up on the screen. As they flicked through in a slideshow, Levi frowned. Most were dark and blurry, and he wasn't sure what he was looking at.

"Most of them seem to be of this particular location," Noah said.

Levi saw metal and water. A factory?

"Where is it?" Chrissy asked.

Noah shook his head. "We're not sure yet."

"Those look like cranes," Chrissy said. "Not small ones, either." The next image made her straighten. "Yes, look. That's a part of a dockside gantry crane."

Noah put his hands on his hips. "You're right."

"Hang on a second." Elle's fingers flew across the screen. "I'm doing a search of all of Sydney's ports. Cross-referencing our drone image database." The comp beeped, and a wide smile lit up Elle's pretty face. "Got it. It's the deep-water port at Botany Bay." Her smile dissolved. "It's right beside Sydney Airport."

Levi stroked his chin. Sydney Airport. That was the Gizzida's base of operations in the area, and where their giant, alien mothership sat.

"So, what's so special about this port?" Tane asked. "Anything that you can see?"

Holmes frowned. "We've documented the port before. As far as we know, it's just empty, rotting docks." The general turned, sliding his hands behind his back.

"Elle, alert Lia that I want the drone team to focus on the port and gather more data. Noah, keep your team studying this parasite. We need to determine why the raptors are focusing on that particular area."

"I can send someone in to scout it out," Santha Cruz said. The head of the intel team was back at work since the birth of her baby.

Holmes shook his head at the brunette. "It's too close to the airport. That will be a last resort."

Levi crossed his arms over his chest. "I have a bad feeling about this." He kept his voice low.

Ash nodded. "I get a bad feeling anytime the aliens are involved."

Ash had been feeling particularly touchy about the raptors, since one of them had shoved a sword through his woman's chest a few weeks back. Thankfully, sweet Marin had survived.

"Stay alert." Holmes' gaze slid around the room, and then stopped on the berserkers. "Squad Three is up for the next mission, so if we find anything we need to act on..."

Tane inclined his head. "We'll be ready."

As others raised their voices to ask questions, Levi looked over at Chrissy.

Only to find her gorgeous red hair missing and her chair empty. Sometime during the briefing, she'd slipped out.

Levi grinned. *You keep running, Spitfire. I'll catch you.*

CHAPTER FOUR

C hrissy leaned over the table in her room, studying the schematics spread out on its surface. She rubbed the back of her neck and breathed deep. She had a candle burning, and its vanilla scent filled the room. She loved her space. After months spent locked in cages by the Gizzida, having some privacy and some nice things that were *hers* meant a lot to her.

Ugly, black memories clawed at her throat, and she breathed in vanilla again. The throaty voice of her favorite singer filtered in from the music speakers. Once the memories receded, she looked at her work again.

She'd been scribbling some ideas for upgrades to the Hunters. Upgrades that would stop those icky alien creatures from infiltrating again. Absently, she rubbed her now-healed wrist.

She needed chocolate. Heading over to the tiny kitchenette, she raided her stash. Some of it was homemade, while a couple of bars had been pilfered from the ruins of the nearby towns. She popped a square of raspberry-infused dark chocolate in her mouth, and took a second to savor the taste.

During those months in captivity, she'd had nothing. No privacy, no bed, no place to call home, no clothes except the rags on her back, and barely enough food to survive. No hope.

There certainly hadn't been any small pleasures, like chocolate.

Every day at the Enclave, she reminded herself of how lucky she was. So many people hadn't made it, and so many people were still raptor prisoners.

Sitting back in her chair, she looked again at the Hunter schematics. She thought of that ugly little octopus creature and rubbed her wrist again, feeling a phantom pain. Doc Emerson, who ran the medical team, had given her a shot of nanomeds. The microscopic medical machines had done their work in a few hours.

And then, her thoughts turned to her rescuer.

No. She wasn't going anywhere near thoughts of him. She did not need Levi King and all his sexy, annoying bikerness in her head.

There was a knock at her door, and happy for the distraction, Chrissy jumped up to open it.

A tall, athletic woman stood on the other side, her dark, red-tinted hair pulled back in a ponytail.

"Hey, Taylor."

"Hi," Taylor Cates answered. "I heard what happened, and thought I'd come and check on you."

"Come on in." Chrissy had been friends with Taylor ever since the Squad Nine soldier had helped rescue

Chrissy and others from the aliens. A faint shiver ran down Chrissy's spine. She was grateful every day that Taylor, and her lover, Devlin, had helped her, little Max, and several others escape.

She held up her block of chocolate and Taylor took it with a grin.

"I'm fine now," Chrissy told her friend. "The nanomeds fixed me right up. But I do *not* want to mess with those icky aliens again."

"Well, I'm glad you were able to kill that thing."

"He's currently being dissected and studied by the medical and tech teams," Chrissy added.

Taylor glanced at the table, and the spread of paperwork and the glowing screen of Chrissy's portable comp.

"I'm working on how to keep these slimy parasites out of my Hunters in the future."

The other woman nodded. "Heard you had some help from a sexy berserker."

Chrissy made a choking sound. "You mean a cocky, arrogant asshole?"

Taylor's lips quirked. "He's all those things, but there is also the hard, muscular body, sexy goatee, hot man bun, mouthwatering tattoos—"

"Hello?" Chrissy coughed and waved a hand in front of her friend's face. "You have a man, remember? A gorgeous, handsome, suave British man."

Taylor grinned, warmth filling her gaze. "I sure do, and I'm not giving him up. But that doesn't mean I can't look at other sexy specimens."

Chrissy studied that warm look on the other woman's face. *Love*. Chrissy had never been in love, and dammit, a part of her was stomp-her-feet-and-pout-in-the-corner envious of Taylor.

"I am a woman with a pulse," Taylor continued, with a wink. "And even though I get to snuggle up with the sexiest, most handsome man in the world every night, Levi King is the kind of bad boy your mother warned you about."

"My mother died young," Chrissy said, "but I don't need anyone to warn me off King. He's arrogant—" she held up her hand, ticking off her fingers "—overconfident, and annoying. Did I mention annoying?"

Taylor's lips twitched. "Maybe. There's a whole lot of protesting going on, though."

Chrissy's eyes bugged out, but before she could retaliate, the ground started to shake. Chrissy gasped and Taylor reached out, gripping the edge of the table.

What the hell?

Chrissy bent her legs to keep her balance, her stomach clenching. Everything in her room rattled and clattered. Something fell off a shelf and broke with a crash.

Taylor gripped Chrissy's arm and pulled her down to the floor. They crawled in under the table.

"Are we under attack?" Chrissy asked.

Taylor tilted her head, her gaze narrowed. "The alarms aren't going off, so I don't think so."

The shaking finally slowed and then stopped. Chrissy looked around the room. "Earthquake?"

Taylor jumped up. "I'll find out. I have to go. I'll catch you later, Chrissy." At a run, the squad soldier was gone, racing out the door.

A curtain of dust fell from a crack in the ceiling and Chrissy coughed.

Then she thought of Max.

Without hesitation, she rushed out the door. The corridor was filled with confused and frightened people.

"Please go back in your rooms," Chrissy called out, keeping her voice calm. "The squads will have everything under control. The general will update us."

"What happened?" someone called out.

"Are the aliens attacking us?"

The aliens had attacked one end of the Enclave a few weeks back and everyone was still jittery.

"The alarms aren't going off," Chrissy repeated Taylor's words. "Everything will be fine." *Please don't make me a liar, universe.*

Chrissy hurried down the hall, stopping to calm a few more people, before she reached the door to Max's foster family. She lifted her hand and knocked.

A moment later, the door opened to show a middle-aged woman, with a makeup-free face and curly, brown hair pulled up in a messy knot on top of her head.

"Hi, Chrissy. So glad to see you." Relief crossed Patricia's face. "Do you know what's going on?" The woman jiggled a sobbing, year-old baby on her hip.

"I don't, but it doesn't appear to be an alien attack. I thought I'd check on you guys. Max?"

Max rushed out and threw his arms around Chrissy's waist. She braced herself to balance his weight. He pressed his dark head against her belly.

She wrapped her arms around him and held him tight. "You okay, big guy?"

The boy nodded and looked up. "Are you?"

Her heart melted. He was such a good kid. After everything he'd been through, he was still always thinking of others.

"I'm okay."

"Ruby is a bit scared, though."

Chrissy glanced through the door, and spied a sweet girl of about three, with cute chubby cheeks, clutching a teddy bear. The girl was usually beaming with a cheeky smile, but there was no sign of that happy expression right now.

Another girl around Max's age was sitting beside Ruby with frightened eyes.

"Come on." Chrissy gripped Max's hand. "Why don't we let Pat sort out the baby, and we'll play a game, or something."

Suddenly, there was the sound of static from the speaker system, and General Holmes' deep voice came across the comms system.

"Your attention, please. Everything is okay. We are not under attack. I repeat, the Enclave is not under attack."

Chrissy let out a long breath.

"So what was that shaking?" Max asked.

"Maybe it was an earthquake," Chrissy said.

Max's bottom lip quivered. "I hate not knowing. Not knowing if it's the aliens."

She pulled him in for a hard hug. She knew what he meant. She'd spent hours in her cell, imagining what terrible things the raptors had planned. Sometimes, not knowing was the worst thing of all.

General Holmes continued to speak with his composed, commanding voice, urging everyone to go about their normal business and stay calm.

"We'll know what happened soon enough," Chrissy said.

But she saw the worry in the boy's eyes. A boy who'd already been through so damn much.

Determination filled her. "I'll find out everything I can and let you know, okay?"

The worry lines bracketing his mouth relaxed. "You promise?"

She crouched to his level. "I promise."

A small smile crossed his face. "You always keep your promises."

"I sure do. Now, how about that game?"

Chrissy stayed with Max's foster family, helping entertain the kids, until they were all smiling again and playing with their toys. Pat and her husband, Jonas, were saints, taking in so many parentless kids and showering them in unrelenting patience and love.

When Chrissy left, she searched for Taylor, but couldn't find the squad soldier anywhere. Damn, she'd been hoping to get some information.

Huffing out a breath, she headed in the direction of the Command Center. Her plan was to find someone to ask for any extra information. But when she reached the glass doors, she saw that the place was full of people, and everyone was distracted and busy.

Then, she spied a tall, muscular man heading down the corridor. His shaggy brown hair, streaked with gold, glinted in the natural lighting system of the Enclave.

"Shaw," Chrissy called out.

Hell Squad's sniper paused and looked over his shoulder. A charming grin tipped his lips up. "Hey, Chrissy."

"Do you know anything about what's going on? Can you tell me anything?"

Shaw's face turned serious. "Holmes is keeping a lid on it until we know for sure. Right now, they're still gathering information."

"It wasn't an earthquake?"

He looked apologetic. "I can't say yet."

So it hadn't been a natural phenomenon, after all. Chrissy gritted her teeth. She *needed* to know. Her imagination was working overtime, her pulse pounding.

She nodded at Shaw. "Thanks anyway."

She turned, striding down the corridor. She decided to check on her Hunters, although she was certain that they'd be fine, parked in their reinforced hangar.

As soon as she entered the bay, she heard the *clang* of a tool hitting metal.

She paused. It was coming from the corner of the space the berserkers used to store their big, upgraded motorcycles. The damn things were covered in armor-plating and weapons. They screamed "apocalypse."

Rounding the line of Hunters, she spied a very fine ass in a worn pair of jeans, and a messy man bun.

Her gaze narrowed. She knew someone who might give her the information she wanted.

And she was going to get it. Now.

LEVI WORKED on the grease line on his bike, not worrying that his hands were covered in the stuff. He was pretty sure he had grease in his veins. His biker name had been Gears for a reason. He was always tinkering with upgrades to make the bikes they used better in the field. Made sense to make them faster and add more firepower.

He set his tool down and grabbed another. For a second, he could almost imagine he was back in the garage behind the Iron Kings clubhouse. He'd turned the club from drugs and prostitution, to designing custom-built bikes and cars. He'd bled and fought to do that, with Ash by his side. They'd made something, and he'd been proud of the name the club was building in custom rides. Proud of the work they'd done.

Then the Gizzida had destroyed it all.

Levi scraped his knuckles on metal and cursed. He watched blood well on his torn skin. Life never made things easy for him and he never expected it would.

"Hey."

He looked up and saw Chrissy striding across the hangar toward him. His gaze slid down her body, looking at the way her dark jeans hugged her curves. Instantly, his cock stirred.

Looking up, he let himself watch the faint jiggle of her breasts as she walked. Well, maybe life gave a little bit of beauty and ease when it suited her.

"I want to know what's going on." She put her hands on her hips.

"Afternoon to you too, Spitfire."

She rolled her eyes. "We both know you don't give a crap about manners."

Levi reached over and grabbed a rag, wiping his hands. "True."

"What was the shaking? Was it an explosion? An earthquake? Were aliens responsible?"

He held up a palm. "I can't say. General will update everyone."

"Levi—"

"Holmes is keeping things under wraps until we know more. Doesn't want people to panic."

Levi watched her blow out a frustrated breath.

"So he's banned you, or anyone, from saying anything?"

"Yeah."

She stepped closer. "You don't care about the rules. You slide under them, step over them, bend them, ignore them, or flat-out just break them."

There was fire in her eyes and it lit up her face. Her cheeks were flushed, and damn, she was something. Her face would look like this if she was spread out on his bed, with him busy working his way down that luscious body.

"Why are you so worked up about this?"

She spun away, her moves jerky. When she looked back, he saw something dark moving through her eyes.

"I was a prisoner. For several long months." Her hands clenched into fists at her sides.

Levi's gut tightened. He knew what she'd been through. He couldn't stand knowing the aliens—bigger, stronger, more powerful—had imprisoned women, children, elderly people. Hell, anyone. He'd always hated bullies, and watching stronger people take advantage of weaker people just because they could made him angry.

A man beating his woman, someone abusing a child, fucking aliens killing and torturing women and children. It all pissed him off.

"I've just come from comforting a small boy who was a prisoner of the raptors. He wants to know what's going on because he's afraid. Every night, he goes to bed, thankful he has a bed, but wondering if the raptors will come and take it away. If he'll end up back in a cage." She pulled in a shuddering breath. "I know that when he gets into his bed tonight, his mind will make up all kinds of crazy situations to explain what happened today."

Something told Levi it wasn't just Max who would be doing that. "You're safe, Chrissy—"

She threw out a hand. "When the lights go out, your brain makes up far worse nightmares of what's hiding in the dark."

Levi had the strange feeling of wanting to chase the darkness away for her. He frowned. *Yeah, you're a regular hero, King.* "The general will share soon."

She huffed out a breath, and then stepped closer until she was pressed against him. Levi found himself with his bike at his back, and an angry woman at his front.

"I don't know why I thought there was a streak of decent under the asshole."

He raised a brow. "You think name-calling will get you what you want? You should have tried a blow job."

Her eyes flared. "You're a dick."

"Yeah. Been called worse." He grabbed her, spinning her until she was pressed against his bike. She squeaked, and he leaned over her, sliding one thigh between hers.

She slammed her hands against his chest. His shirt was unbuttoned and her fingers touched his skin.

"I do follow the rules, Chrissy. Mine."

Her chest was heaving, her gorgeous breasts pressing upward. Damn, he wanted to see them bare. See what shade of pink her nipples were, and run his mouth all over them.

Her hands flexed on his chest, and he saw her gaze drop to his pecs, then his abs. He smiled. "I can see how much you want me."

Her gaze flicked up, a stubborn look settling on her face. "Screw you."

"Yeah," he continued. "I see you wondering how my hands would feel on you." He moved his hand, letting his fingers drift down her arm. They left a faint smudge of grease on her skin.

"You have no shame," she ground out.

"No. And I know you're wondering how my lips would feel on that honey-smooth skin of yours. Maybe closing over one of your hard nipples."

"You're delusional."

"You can't lie to me," he murmured.

All of a sudden, her hands slid downward. When they reached his belly, he sucked in a breath.

"You have nothing I want, King."

"Liar, liar." He closed one hand over her breast, rolling her nipple between his fingers. Her lips parted and her hips shifted. Then she sank her teeth into her bottom lip.

"You're wondering how my cock would feel sliding

into you." His voice was a husky growl. "How much I'd stretch you out."

"Asshole." Her voice was husky too. She pushed against him. "Let me go."

Levi knew no one would ever accuse him of having polished manners, but they'd also never accuse him of taking a woman against her will. Even if the woman in question did want him.

He stepped back and her legs dropped back to the ground. She put her hands down to slide off his bike.

"Damn." She yanked her hand away from the bike. When she lifted it, he saw blood on her finger.

"What did you do?"

"Nothing. Just a small cut." Shooting him a venomous look, she strode past him and back toward her Hunters.

"Chrissy?"

She paused, but didn't look back.

"Sleep with the light on tonight."

She was silent for a second. "It doesn't stop the nightmares." She strode away.

Levi shoved his hands on his hips and watched her go. His cock was hard as a rock, but it was the other unfamiliar emotions churning in his gut that he wasn't so sure about.

CHAPTER FIVE

G od, she must be losing her mind.

Chrissy stomped over to her toolbox and wrenched it open. She was mad at herself. Not just because she'd touched Levi King...but because she wanted to do it again.

She rummaged around in her tools and found a clean rag to wipe her bleeding finger. She shouldn't go anywhere near him. He was too arrogant, too cocky...and too sexy and tempting.

Ugh. What was she thinking? The man had bedded half of the Enclave's single ladies. She had no desire to be a notch on a bedpost. All she wanted was information, and for some dumb reason, she'd thought he'd give it to her.

Ignoring her stinging finger, she opened the hood of the Hunter. *Work.* She needed to work.

Pulling her rolling toolbox closer, she leaned over, studying the Hunter's engine. Bec had finished printing a few of the parts Chrissy needed. Time to start putting her baby back together and get the Hunter operational.

Chrissy pulled out her auto socket wrench and got to work loosening bolts. The whizzing sound it made as she worked on a particularly stubborn bolt was soothing.

Clink. She turned her head, and spied two bottles of beer resting on her toolbox, along with a tiny first aid kit.

She swiveled her head and looked back at Levi.

"Let me look at your finger."

She glared at him. "It's fine."

He glanced at where her hand rested on the Hunter and raised a brow. There was blood smeared on the metal.

He seized her hand. "It needs cleaning." He grabbed a beer and handed it to her. Then he opened the first aid kit.

Not sure how to deal with this sudden kindness, Chrissy took a long sip of the beer.

She watched Levi's big hands as he carefully started cleaning the cut on her finger. It was minor. As a mechanic, she'd had plenty of cuts and scrapes. Her hands were covered in small scars that the nanomeds had deemed too inconsequential to heal.

Expertly, Levi applied some cream and then placed a bandage over the scrape. "Tell me about the Gizzida prison."

She stiffened. "You want me to relive the worst moments of my life?"

"The past is there, whether you talk about it or not. Seems to me that it's eating at you. Might be better to offload some of it."

She took another sip of beer. *What the hell.* If he wanted to know all her dark, ugly memories, fine. "I'd been on the run since the invasion. I was in Australia on vacation at the time, so I didn't know anyone."

"You're American?"

She nodded. "From Miami. I spent the first few months scavenging, and moving around with other small groups of survivors." She'd watched many of them get picked off by the raptors or die. "The last group I was with had lots of older people and kids. We had a few camps we moved between bushland north of Sydney." Her throat tightened. "Six months we survived, before a raptor patrol caught us."

She closed her eyes, and in her head, she heard the echoes of the screams and the guttural grunts of the aliens. She felt scaly claws grab her, and the rough treatment as they jerked her around.

"We were shoved in some alien vehicles and taken to an alien factory." She cleared her throat to loosen the lump in it. "You know the rest. We ended up in the bowels of the factory in cages—" she glanced up at him "—and we were used as test subjects for their alien tech. Mainly the *oura* globe. They'd use it on us, over and over again."

A muscle ticked in Levi's jaw. "Not a big fan of bastards who torture women and children."

"I'm not a big fan of people who torture anyone." Chrissy tilted her head. "I thought motorcycle gangs did whatever they pleased, and are...pretty violent."

He shrugged a broad shoulder. "Motorcycle club, not a gang. We worked hard. Partied harder. And yeah, things used to get pretty physical, but we never hurt women or children."

He might annoy her, but she believed him. He could be a cocky prick, but he went out there every day and risked his own life and fought for their safety.

"Besides, I'm not in a motorcycle club anymore. I'm just a soldier."

Chrissy lifted her beer. Levi King was not *just* anything.

She scanned his rugged face, with his sexy goatee, and the faint lines around his gold-brown eyes that said he was a man who laughed and lived. "Whatever happened earlier to make the ground shake wasn't good."

Levi took a sip of his own beer. "Nope."

His intense gaze moved over her face, and then set his beer down, muttering something about chasing away the darkness. She frowned, wondering what the hell he was talking about.

He straightened. "The Gizzida set off a massive explosion that flooded part of Sydney, near the airport. It completely submerged a port and the surrounding suburbs."

***

LEVI WATCHED Chrissy frown as she absorbed the information. "Why?"

"Million-dollar question." He grabbed his beer again.

"So they flooded a section of the city?"

He nodded. "Mostly the port right near their mother-ship at the airport."

She nibbled on her lip, and he watched the movement, imagining how those pink lips would look stretched around his cock.

"They're hiding something," Chrissy said.

"Yep. Don't know what. Holmes will update us once he knows more." Levi cocked his head. "And now you have more questions than answers. More fodder for those nightmares. That's why the general didn't want to share yet." Maybe there were other ways Levi could help her forget those dark memories.

"Maybe, but I still prefer knowing something over nothing. I...appreciate you telling me."

He cupped her chin. "Say it again."

Her gaze narrowed. "You heard me."

"No, don't think I did."

"I don't think I like you."

She was such a challenge—an irresistible one. "Drink your beer."

She lifted her chin. "Why?"

"Because you'll need the energy when I bend you over the hood of this Hunter and fuck you."

She straightened like she'd been electrocuted. "You just can't help yourself. You have to be an annoying asshole."

"So you keep telling me." Levi stepped closer, until his chest brushed hers. "Tell me you don't want me to do it."

A frustrated look twisted her face, but triumph flared in him. He saw bright, hot desire in those pretty eyes.

She shook her head. "Why don't you go find one of your bed buddies—"

"Don't want anyone else. I want you." He leaned down, his nose brushing her cheek. "I wanna fuck you, Chrissy, and you know you'll love it."

"I don't like anything about you."

He backed her up until she bumped into the Hunter. "You're lying now. You want me, Spitfire. You want me lodged deep."

He expected her to shove him backward and go for her wrench. But of course, Chrissy surprised him.

She hooked her fingers in the belt of his jeans and yanked him forward.

"If you tell anyone," she whispered fiercely, "I'll hit you with my hammer."

He felt fingers reach for his zipper. *Fuck.* He leaned in and kissed her.

As he thrust his tongue inside her sweet mouth, he wrapped his arms around her. She tasted like beer, and, for some weird reason, raspberries.

Damn, Levi had always had a thing for raspberries.

She pulled back. "No kissing, King. Just fucking." She pushed at his shirt and it slid off. Her hands ran over his chest, and she made a small humming noise. Then she leaned forward, licking one of his nipples. She found his nipple ring and tugged it with her teeth.

All the blood in his body rushed south. His cock swelled, and desire was a fierce punch to his gut. He reached past her and slammed the hood of the Hunter down. Then he gripped her hips and lifted her until she rested on the hood.

It took him seconds to yank her tank top off. He couldn't help but stare at her gorgeous, full breasts cupped by black lace. *Fucking hell.* As he got rid of her bra, she leaned down, her mouth on his neck. She bit him, hard, and Levi groaned. Then her breasts were bare and he had to taste them. He pushed her back a little, then buried his face in her sweet curves. He sucked one nipple, and felt her hands slide into his hair.

"I like it harder, biker man." Her voice was husky.

He scraped his teeth on her nipple and sucked hard, sending her writhing against him. He worked on the other nipple while he unsnapped her jeans. Then he stripped them off her.

Damn gorgeous. He was one lucky man. He stared at her for a second, absorbing the picture of a naked Chrissy on the black metal of the Hunter.

He had to be inside her. *Now.*

He spun her around, watching as she pressed her cheek to the metal. Her naked ass was on perfect display and he cupped it, squeezing her soft cheeks. She moaned.

"You want me, Spitfire?"

She pushed back into his hands. Need was a pounding drive inside him. He slid his fingers between her thighs and stroked her folds. "You're fucking soaked."

She rode his hand. "Just fuck me."

Oh, yeah. He wanted this woman like he couldn't remember wanting anyone before. He reached down and freed his aching cock. He wanted to be inside her, and he needed to douse the flames licking at his gut.

He leaned over her body, rubbing his cock against the crack of her ass. "Say my name, Spitfire."

She made a frustrated noise. "Stop talking and fuck me."

He gripped her hips. "You have a contraceptive implant?"

She nodded her head.

"Now, say my name, and I'll make you come so hard you'll feel it for a week."

Hot eyes glared back at him. "Never pegged you for all talk and no action."

Enflamed, Levi thrust forward and slammed his cock inside her.

Her cry echoed through the hangar and his jaw clenched. *Fuck.* She was so fucking tight and wet.

Chrissy made another strangled noise and then shoved back against him.

"I'm still not screaming your name yet, King."

Cheeky, mouthy tease. He slid out, and then thrust back in. As he started fucking her, pleasure roared through him, and he felt the driving need to hear her come screaming his name.

He picked up speed. Levi was a man who always got what he wanted.

CHAPTER SIX

C hrissy was panting, her hands pressed hard against the cool metal of the Hunter.

God, he was so deep. She was so full of Levi King.

He leaned over her, his lips at her ear. "Say my name, Spitfire."

She shoved back against him. "Just be quiet and do this."

He pulled out, and the blunt head of his cock rubbed against her, teasing her. She made a strangled sound. Damn, he was a tease. Then he buried himself inside her, and they both groaned. She felt his hands biting into the skin of her hips.

"You are so damn tight," he growled.

She arched her back. "Stop talking."

He pulled out until only the head of his cock was notched inside her. She bit down on her lip to stop the moan of protest escaping.

"Say my name."

"No."

He slid back in, nudging something inside her that made her moan in pleasure.

He pulled back out again, taking away that fabulous cock. "Say. My. Name."

"So damn arrogant—"

"Spitfire," he growled and pulled out. This time, it was his fingers that pumped back inside her.

God. She bit down hard on her lip to stop from begging him.

He slid his fingers in and out. His thumb brushed her clit, and this time, the moan escaped.

"Soaked. And this ass." He squeezed one globe. "Perfection."

"You're...supposed to be fucking me."

His hands slid away, and again, she felt the thick head of his cock running through her folds. "You know what you have to do."

Damn the man. She looked back over her shoulder. "Fuck me, Levi. Hard."

He slammed back inside her. There was no rhythm or skill, just hard, powerful thrusts. It was wild dominance, and God help her, she loved it.

Her moans turned to cries. She was on fire and it felt so good. There was no darkness, worry, or fear, just pleasure. She slid her hand down beneath her body until she found her clit.

"Yeah, baby, stroke that clit," he said. "Damn, you're so sexy."

She stroked herself, sensations gathering inside her. She couldn't think, could only feel. For the first time in so long, since the aliens invaded—hell, maybe longer—she felt so good and so free.

"I feel you tightening around my cock. Come for me now, Chrissy."

"Oh, I'm close."

He thrust back inside her, harder and faster.

"Come for me, Spitfire. Milk my cock while you touch yourself."

Damn man knew exactly what he was doing to her. "I don't like you," she panted.

"Yes, you do." With each thrust, expulsions of air escaped his chest.

Chrissy felt her orgasm coming in like a huge wave. Her body tensed.

"Say my name." A hot, possessive whisper in her ear.

But Chrissy was too far gone. Her release exploded inside her. She turned her head and bit down on his forearm to muffle her scream.

Then she let herself drown in the pleasure.

LEVI KEPT THRUSTING, listening to the sexy sounds Chrissy made as she came. Damn, she was sexy as hell.

He'd had a lot of sex with a lot of women, but as pleasure clamped down on him and he kept driving into Chrissy's tight body, he knew he hadn't had sex like this.

She was still shoving back against him, meeting his thrusts. Giving as much as she took.

Challenging him to the end.

He thrust deep into her, and as his release rolled through him, he groaned and poured himself inside her. *Jesus.*

He collapsed on her, trying to catch his breath. But before he could do that, Chrissy shifted beneath him, nudging him back. He stepped back, pulling out of her. He had a second to appreciate the sight of her sprawled on the Hunter, perfect ass in the air.

Fuck. He'd never seen anything hotter.

And when he saw his come leaking down her thighs, he knew he was wrong. The sight of *that* was the hottest thing he'd ever seen. He smiled. Marked by him.

Chrissy turned, cool as an ice queen looking down on her subjects. She snatched up her clothes and started yanking them on.

"You mention this to anyone, I'll skewer you with my laser cutter."

His spitfire was back. Watching her dress made his cock stir again. "You didn't say my name when you came."

Her gaze flicked up to his. "You'll get over it."

"You will scream it next time."

The hand stilled on the zipper of her jeans. "There won't be a next time, King."

"Yes, there will."

"No." She pushed her hair off her face. "This was a one-shot deal."

"Yes, there will," he said emphasizing his words and stepping closer to her.

She tensed, watching him like he was a wild animal. He leaned in, making sure his lips brushed her ear lobe.

"I want to eat you and taste your honey on my tongue. I want your thighs wrapped around my head while I suck your clit."

Her chest hitched and his gaze dropped to her breasts.

"And those fabulous breasts deserve some more attention."

She shook her head and retied her hair.

"I want to watch you wrap your pretty lips around my cock."

"Shut up." She jerked away from him, tugging on the hem of her tank top. "It's not happening again."

"You will scream my name when I make you come. I always get what I want."

She rolled her eyes. "God, get over—"

Something beeped in his pocket and she paused.

Levi cursed, pulling his jeans closed and sliding his communicator from his pocket. He knew it had to be important because it was late and he was off-duty. He thumbed the device.

"You got Levi."

"Levi." It was Indy. "Holmes has called an emergency meeting. He has intel on the submerged port."

Levi saw Chrissy's head shoot up.

"You got it, Indy," he answered. "On my way."

"I've already called the others. Now I just need to find Chrissy Hagan. The general asked that she attend too."

Levi's eyebrows shot up. "I just saw her in the

Hunter hanger. She was making a lot of noise, so it was hard to miss her."

Chrissy's eyes widened and she glared at him.

"Good. Can you tell her—"

"I'll tell her she's needed," he told Indy.

"Awesome," Indy replied. "Thanks Levi. See you in the Command Center."

CHAPTER SEVEN

C hrissy followed Levi down the corridor, her body still tingling.

What the hell had she been thinking?

She'd let Levi King bend her over a Hunter and bang her brains out. Even now, she could smell him—that dark musk—and feel the press of cool metal under her cheek as he powered inside her with that big cock. As she walked, her damp thighs rubbed together, and her still-swollen lady parts were more than happy.

Jeez. Staring straight ahead, she refused to look at him. He didn't talk and neither did she. But she made herself a silent promise that she wouldn't touch him again. Ever.

They rounded the corridor leading into the Command Center and Chrissy prayed she didn't have sex hair. The glass doors opened, and inside, she saw the other squad members had already gathered for the meeting. Levi grabbed her hand and pulled her into the room.

"Let go," she growled, trying to pull away from him, but he held tight.

"Levi." Ash waved them over.

Chrissy didn't miss the way the other man's gaze dropped to their linked hands. She tugged again, and this time, managed to get free.

Chrissy quickly spun away. She needed some space from Levi. He was like a magnet, or a whirlpool…no, a black hole. He pulled her in, against her better judgement, like a vortex she couldn't escape.

God, she'd let him fuck her. And it had been the best sex of her life. She was so screwed.

She quickly found a space not far from Squad Nine, and leaned against the wall.

"Okay, let's get started." General Holmes' voice rang out over the room.

Everyone quieted.

"The drone team has been working overtime to explore the flooded area at Port Botany." Holmes nodded to a pretty redhead, with hair a few shades darker than Chrissy's, standing nearby. Lia was head of the drone team. "And the tech team also sent in a small spiderbot on one of the drones."

The big wall of screens filled with images. Chrissy paused, staring at the submerged port. She could see giant cranes tilted over, protruding from the water like dead branches.

What the hell were the aliens up to? One screen was filled with video footage. It showed a line of alien trikes approaching the submerged area. She eyed the rugged, black vehicles, each with their three big spikes mounted on the front.

Chrissy had a small collection of parts off the alien trikes that she'd accumulated. She played with them in her free time, to see what she could use. The mix of organic and tech was fascinating, but creepy as hell. She figured that the more they understood the alien vehicles, the better chance they had of using that information against the raptors.

Then she saw something else at the end of the alien convoy. She leaned forward. God, it was massive. This had to be the steg that Levi had mentioned. Holy cow, it was huge, and she would hate to see that saw headed in her direction. Her hands itched to see inside its engine. It was ugly, but it clearly packed a lot of grunt and power.

The vehicles were headed straight for the water, and they weren't slowing down. She frowned. A makeshift ramp had been fashioned from ruined concrete and sheets of metal. One by one, the vehicles drove down the ramp and *into* the water.

"What the hell?" she heard Levi mutter.

"They are definitely hiding something under there that they don't want us to see," Tane said quietly.

Chrissy tapped her foot on the floor. The Hunters could withstand a lot, but they certainly weren't waterproof. She wanted to know exactly how the aliens sealed their vehicles to be watertight, and how their engines worked under the water. That was info she could use.

Holmes nodded. "The spiderbot was able to go into the water. Let's see the footage." He inclined his head at Elle at her workstation.

Another screen filled with wobbly video. It showed a glimpse of tiny, metal legs, as the spiderbot skittered across the ground. They watched it plunge into the water and darkness filled the screen. It took a few seconds, but shapes appeared in the gloom. In the distance, an orange light shone in the murkiness.

The spiderbot started zooming forward, moving through the water quickly.

The alien convoy came into view, traveling slowly down the submerged ramp. She spotted the back of the steg, with its unique armor plates sticking up off its roof. It had no problem driving through the water.

"Ahh, shit," a gravelly voice clipped out.

Chrissy glanced at Marcus Steele's scarred face. The man looked very unhappy. She turned back to the screen, and that's when she realized what it was they were all looking at. There was a huge orange dome under the water.

"What is it?" she asked.

Lots of gazes moved her way, and she was sure they were wondering why she was at this meeting, surrounded by squad soldiers. She was wondering as well.

When she saw Levi looking at her with a half-smile, like he was thinking of what they'd done on the Hunter, she quickly looked away, heat in her cheeks.

"We destroyed a dome like this one in the Hunter Valley," Marcus said. "It had an alien lab in it."

She grimaced. An alien lab with poor humans trapped inside, being transformed into aliens in giant tanks. Staring at the screen, she watched as the spiderbot got closer to the dome. The alien vehicles moved toward a large doorway in the side of the dome.

"It's heavily guarded," a deep voice said. It belonged to Roth Masters, leader of Squad Nine. "Lots of weapons lining the door."

"And look," Roth's second, Mac Carides pointed, "there are raptor patrols in the water."

The humanoid raptor aliens came into view. Chrissy frowned. These ones were different than the regular raptors—more streamlined, with a different-shaped head.

"They've been bred for the water," Marcus said with a scowl.

God, was it possible that these raptors could breathe under the water? She saw they were holding small propulsion devices that moved them through the water quickly and easily.

"Shit," Mac said. "What was that?"

A dark shadow sliced through the water, just out of clear view. Whatever it was, it was big.

Marcus and Roth traded a weighted look. "Probably the aquatic alien we encountered last time we entered this area."

"We'll just have to feed it Shaw again," Marcus' second, Cruz, murmured with a grin.

The sniper smiled. "It was no match for me."

Beside him, Claudia snorted. "Maybe it choked." She tilted her head. "But I am rather partial to you now, so perhaps we can come up with another plan."

On the screen, the bot started swimming along the dome, doing a lap.

Lia moved forward. "We've analyzed the footage of

the dome. There appears to be only one way inside, and that's through the door that the vehicles used."

"We need to know what the hell the Gizzida are doing in there," Holmes said.

Chrissy stared back at the screen, an idea forming. They had to get in that thing. It was risky...

She thought of Max. He deserved a chance at a real life.

"How the hell are we going to do that?" Levi muttered.

Her heart thumped. Yeah, she had an idea. *But would it work?*

When she looked up, she saw that General Holmes was looking at her.

LEVI STARED at the orange dome. He had a bad feeling about this. In the Iron Kings, his instincts had saved the club too many times to count. He often threw caution to the wind and went strictly with his gut.

The aliens were done messing around with humanity. They were getting serious.

Whatever the raptors were hiding in that dome wasn't going to be good, and they had to get in there and see. Getting into a heavily protected, underwater dome wasn't going to be a walk in the park.

"I can get you in there."

Chrissy's voice made Levi stiffen. *What the fuck?*

He looked at her, taking in her messy hair. Hair he'd messed up from having his hands in it while he'd fucked her. Instantly, he thought about being balls deep inside her. She was so damn tight, and those luscious curves of hers... He hadn't come that hard in a long time. Hell, ever.

Holmes nodded. "I'm listening."

Levi's attention snapped back to the conversation at hand.

"I can get you an alien vehicle. You can use that to get inside." She shoved her hands in the pockets of her jeans. "A squad can drive right in."

Levi watched the general's chiseled face, and realized this was exactly why Chrissy had been invited to this meeting. Holmes was smart, always one step ahead.

It pissed Levi off. "How the hell can you get a vehicle?" he snapped.

Chrissy's head whipped around, her auburn ponytail flying. She glared at him. "I need to sabotage a trike and steal it. It'll take me a bit to work out how to operate it, but I've been studying the remnants of one, and I have a basic understanding."

"Sabotage an alien vehicle..." Levi went still, considering just how up close and personal she'd need to get.

Chrissy nodded, looking back at Holmes. "I'll need a squad to take me into the field. I need to lie in wait for a trike. If someone can cause a distraction, I can get under one of these alien vehicles and disable it."

Levi's hands clenched into fists. She wanted to go into the field? Into a fucking firefight and climb under an alien vehicle?

"That is a fucking bad idea," he growled.

Her eyes narrowed. "It's a fucking brilliant idea."

"I agree with her," Holmes said.

"What?" Levi spun. He wanted to punch something, preferably Holmes' perfect face. "She's not made to be out there."

"Screw you, King. I can do this. And I was out there for months with those damn aliens. I want to help, or we might all end up dead anyway."

Damn. He had to admit the woman had balls, even if her idea made him crazy.

"Levi." Tane's quiet voice. His squad leader gripped Levi's shoulder. "Cool it."

Holmes cleared his throat. "I'll select a squad to accompany Chrissy into the field—"

"If she sets foot outside the Enclave, Squad Three is with her." Levi didn't give a fuck what the orders were.

The general scowled. "I give the orders around here, King."

Chrissy stood, her glare white-hot on Levi. "You have no claim over me."

"Yes, I fucking do," he goaded her. He sure as hell wasn't shy or discreet. He was more than happy to tell people exactly what they'd done on that Hunter if he had to.

An annoyed look dominated her face, and she crossed her arms over her chest. Levi could feel his squad mates staring at him, no doubt wondering what the hell he was doing. Out of the corner of his eye, he saw Ash looking at the ceiling and trying to hide a smile. He was doing a piss-poor job of it.

"We'd like to protect Chrissy," Tane said.

Holmes nodded. "Fine. Plan it out. Get us an alien vehicle."

The meeting was over and the crowd started to disperse.

Chrissy shot Levi a look that should set him on fire and stomped toward the door.

"If you're trying to get into her bunk," Tane said in a bland tone, "this is a fucked-up way of going about it."

"She is *pissed*," Ash added cheerfully.

Levi didn't care. She'd be protected, no matter what. "She sets foot outside this base, the berserkers have her back."

Tane nodded. "Okay, so let's plan this sabotage mission."

CHAPTER EIGHT

Twenty-four hours later, Levi was still stewing over Chrissy and the mission. He slammed his locker door closed with a loud bang that didn't soothe any of his dissatisfaction.

He'd helped Tane plan the mission. It was a typical, slightly crazy berserker mission...and he didn't want Chrissy anywhere near it.

He lifted his carbine and checked it over with practiced ease. He was still shirtless, but decked out in his lower-body armor, carbon fiber molded over his cargo pants.

He was taking Chrissy into enemy territory, to sabotage and steal an alien vehicle. *Fuck.*

Memories drifted into his head, just as they when he'd been lying alone in his bed last night. Chrissy, gloriously naked, bent over that Hunter. Her tight little body taking him, and her cries echoing in his ears.

Levi blew out a breath and focused. All around him

in their squad locker room, his squad mates were getting prepped. Tane and Ash were already in full armor, checking their weapons. Dom was sitting quietly in the corner, checking his knives. Hemi was still slapping armor on. Griff was mostly naked. Levi's gaze snagged on the man's bare back and some wicked scars. A ragged one ran down beside the man's spine, before heading for his side. Levi guessed he'd gotten it in prison. It was hard for a cop to survive on the other side, trapped among the people they'd helped send to prison. But Levi knew that Griff was tough to the bone —and he'd gone inside well-trained and knowing what to expect.

Chrissy wasn't trained. She was going out there and had to know there was a chance she'd end up dead or captured.

Levi grabbed his upper armor and slammed it into place.

"Bro, you need to dial the anger down a notch." Ash appeared beside him.

"Not gonna happen."

His best friend rolled his eyes. "We'll take care of her. I know you're interested in her, but from the way she glares at you, I don't think you're in, yet."

"I was in when I was balls deep inside her," Levi growled. Shit, he could still taste and smell her. She was the prettiest, freshest, and sexiest thing he'd ever had. She stood up to him at every turn, challenged him, and sure as hell lit a firestorm inside him.

Ash's eyebrows rose. "She slept with you?"

Levi smiled darkly. "There was no sleeping, brother."

Then his smile dissolved. "Once. It was one wild, angry fuck. I want more." *A lot more.*

"Let's roll," Tane called out, swinging his carbine over his shoulder.

Everyone grabbed their weapons, and together, the berserkers headed out into the corridor.

A woman ran up the hall, almost skipping. Marin made a beeline for Ash and leaped into the air, trusting him to catch her. Levi watched his friend catch his woman and swing her in close for a kiss.

"Be careful out there," Marin said.

"I will," Ash promised, his gaze soft.

Levi felt his shoulders tighten. He wondered what it was like to have someone who truly gave a damn whether you lived or died.

"Hello, ladies," Indy drawled through their earpieces. "I'm testing our comm line, and then it's time to get your mighty fine, armor-clad asses on a Hawk."

Griff growled. "That woman has no respect."

When they turned into the Hawk hangar, Levi saw maintenance team members rushing around and prepping the lead Hawk. The quadcopter was made of dull, gray metal, with four shrouded rotors. Fast, maneuverable, and tough, they'd been the backbone of humanity's fight against the aliens.

But Levi's eyes barely took the Hawk in before settling on the redhead waiting beside it.

She was wearing armor, and talking with Taylor, one of the Squad Nine soldiers. The other woman was talking intently, giving Chrissy tips or a lecture—Levi couldn't be sure. When Taylor lifted her head and spotted the berserkers, she quickly leaned forward and hugged Chrissy, before she hurried away.

As Levi reached her, Chrissy turned to face him and lifted her chin. She looked composed and calm, with several tools strapped to her belt. Cool as a fucking ice cube.

"Ready, Chrissy?" Tane asked.

"As ready as I'll ever be," she answered.

The side door of the Hawk slid open, and a man's face appeared, topped by pale, shaggy hair. "Welcome to Erickson Air. I'm Finn, and I'll be your pilot today."

Finn Erickson, Hawk pilot extraordinaire, smiled at them. When his gaze fell on Chrissy, his smile widened.

Levi frowned. The man was lucky that Levi knew he had his own redhead—Lia from the drone team.

As the others climbed aboard, Levi grabbed Chrissy's arm. She looked back at him.

"I've got something for you," he said.

She shot him a suspicious look. "You have nothing I want."

He gripped her arm more firmly and she tugged against his hold. He pulled her close and caught her scent. Something sweet with an undertone of the engine oil from the Hunters. He liked it.

"Now I know you're lying. I bet if I stripped that armor off you, your hard nipples and damp panties would prove you wrong."

Her eyes flared. "Screw you—"

"You already did. You still feel me between your legs, Spitfire?"

Chrissy straightened. "We have a *mission*."

"We do. And I'll keep you safe out there."

"I can look after myself, King."

"I know." He handed over the laser pistol he'd grabbed for her. "This is for you. It's probably a little too big for you, but I know you can handle it. It packs a punch, just like you do."

She stared at the weapon.

"Just in case," he said.

"Thanks," she said grudgingly, as she took it.

"It's all charged up. Just point and shoot."

She nodded. "I haven't used this particular model before, but I've done some shooting in the past."

"Good."

Together, they turned to the Hawk. Levi gripped her waist and lifted her aboard. He leaped in after her, and watched her strap into a seat.

His gaze went to the cramped back of the Hawk. Two of the modified bikes they used were crammed in the back—his and Tane's. A second Hawk would be dropping off Dom's and Griff's. These bikes had little in common with the Harleys and custom rides he'd worked on before the invasion. These babies were covered in armor-plating and weapons.

Soon, the squad was settled and Finn's voice came from the cockpit.

"Everyone, please take your seats, and strap in or find a handhold. We're all out of peanuts and pretzels, and the flight attendants will *not* be around to serve drinks, but sit back and enjoy the ride anyway."

Seconds later, the quadcopter lifted off, traveling up through a vertical tube cut into the rock. Then, they cleared the opening and there was nothing around them but blue sky.

As the Hawk turned and zoomed forward, Tane turned to face them. He was standing, holding a hand-hold above his head.

"I'm gonna recap this once more. We're heading to a road that we know the alien vehicles patrol, just north of here. It's secluded and surrounded by trees. They usually pass through pretty fast and don't stop."

Levi knew that there was something in the trees that the raptors reacted to and disliked. The geek squad was still trying to work out exactly what that was. They knew the alien canid dogs hated cedar oil, but still hadn't determined what affected the raptors.

"Let's go over the steps again," Tane said. "We find a spot on the road and dig a hole in the center. Like a hunting blind that we can camouflage."

And like hunters, they'd wait patiently inside for their prey.

"Chrissy, Levi, and Hemi will hide inside," Tane continued. "The rest of us have the job of making sure an alien vehicle stops right over the hole."

"How?" Chrissy asked.

It was Dom who leaned forward, his dark eyes as black as night. The slightest smile tilted his lips. "Explosives."

Chrissy shook her head. "Right. The berserkers don't do anything subtly, do they?"

Tane ignored her muttered comment. "Once we get the vehicle stopped, Chrissy pops up beneath it, and works her magic to sabotage it. Those of us providing the distraction will take off on the bikes into the trees. We want the aliens to follow us, and willingly abandon the vehicle that's not working. We can't have them knowing that we have appropriated it."

There were nods all around.

"Coming up to the landing zone," Finn called out.

Levi watched Chrissy's hands clench together. Now, he could see the hints of nerves. She was heading back into alien-controlled territory. She knew there was a chance she could be captured again.

Her gaze flicked up and she spotted him watching her. She lifted her chin.

She'd do it. There was steel under those curves, a confidence he found irresistible, a courage that scared the shit out of him. There was no way she was going to let the aliens win.

And Levi was going to make sure she was back, safe and sound, in the Enclave by nightfall.

CHRISSY'S BOOTS HIT DIRT, and she glanced back at the hovering quadcopter, watching the rest of the berserkers leap off with practiced ease.

Her borrowed armor felt awkward and unfamiliar, but from the scars and scratches on the men's gear, she knew wearing armor was as familiar as breathing for them.

The second Hawk appeared, hovering beside the first one, and the berserkers worked fast, setting up makeshift ramps and rolling the bikes out. She'd seen the big, modified bikes loads of times, parked in a corner of the Hunter hangar. But she'd never seen them in action.

As the Hawks lifted off in a silent gust of air, she felt a rush of nerves. This was it. Even if she wanted to, it was too late to change her mind. She wasn't safe behind the sturdy walls of the Enclave.

Swallowing hard, she took in their surroundings. Trees, a dirt road, and overgrown grass growing through a tumbled-down wire fence. It was too easy to remember the raptors chasing her through several yards of abandoned houses. She'd almost lost them, but they'd caught her scaling a fence. Her gloved fingers curled. Right now, she felt horribly exposed. Her chest tightened, and she tried to drag in some breaths. She *so* didn't need a panic attack right now.

A raptor isn't going to jump out from behind a tree, Chrissy.

She fingered her tools. Besides, she was surrounded by berserkers. She let her gaze linger on each one of them. Tane scanned around with his composed face. Beside him, Hemi stood, cradling his carbine and smiling. But she didn't miss the serious glint in his dark eyes. Griff had already sat on his bike, his gaze on the trees. Dom stood just behind Griff, and was turning a knife over in his gloved hand.

Then she looked at Ash and Levi. It was almost possible to sense the closeness between the two men. She'd heard they'd grown up like brothers, and had run the Iron Kings together. They had a slightly different edge to the other berserkers. One that said they fought hard and partied harder.

"Squad Three," Indy's voice came over the comm line. "You have thirty minutes until the alien vehicles are due."

"Acknowledged," Tane murmured.

"Helmet on." Levi appeared and brushed the neck of her armor. The retractable helmet slid into place, covering her hair.

"Thanks." She could do this. She was *determined* to do this. To give the survivors—to give Max—a chance.

She heard a rustling noise in the grass and she started. She turned to see a kangaroo jump out of the trees. It stared at them for a moment, then it bounded over the broken fence and hopped away.

Her shoulders sagged.

"Hey." Levi cupped her chin and tilted it up. "You've got this."

She swallowed. "I know. Just some bad memories resurfacing."

He stroked her cheek. "I'm not letting any alien fucker close to you. And I'm definitely not letting them take you."

Something inside her trembled. It had been a long time since someone had looked out for her. Even before the invasion, she'd worked hard to pull her weight at the garage, and prove herself to her dad and make things easier for him. The rest of the time she'd spent cleaning up her sister's messes.

Levi could be infuriating sometimes, but on this, she believed him one-hundred percent.

"You've got the pistol I gave you," he said. "That's

backup if you need it. But I'm going to do my best to make sure you don't."

Damn, she hated when he was nice and thoughtful. "Thanks. Levi...I mean it."

Suddenly, he leaned down and pressed his lips to hers. It wasn't a long or deep kiss, and before she could react, he lifted his head. "You've got this."

God, had Levi King just comforted her? She nodded and glanced at the others. Jeez, they were all avidly watching them. Of course, these were men who made no pretense at having manners or tact. Tane's face was its usual blank mask, Griff and Dom looked curious, and Ash and Hemi were flat-out grinning.

"Okay," Tane said, swinging a leg over his bike. "Mount up. We'll ride along the road until we find the best place for an ambush."

Hemi climbed on behind his brother, Ash sat behind Griff, and Dom was solo on his own bike. Levi climbed on his bike with a flex of his thighs and patted the seat behind him.

"You're with me, babe."

She climbed on, refusing to admit she was a teeny bit excited to ride the bike. "Don't 'babe' me." She gingerly gripped his armor-clad body.

Levi revved the engine. "You'd better hold on tighter than that."

She saw Tane speed away, the others following. A cloud of dust rose into the air. Apparently, the berserkers didn't do slow. She tightened her hold.

And Levi took off.

Chrissy clamped her arms around him, the wind rushing into her face.

Oh. God.

Exhilaration filled her. She loved the safety of the Enclave, but she had to admit, she missed the wind in her face sometimes. And the chance to *move*.

Levi took a corner fast, leaning them into the turn, and she leaned with him. They caught up with the others, the engine of the big bike throbbing beneath them. She tightened her legs on Levi, feeling the heat of his hard body.

Soon, Tane pulled them to a stop on a straight stretch of the road shadowed by trees.

Levi braked hard and Chrissy was pushed against him. He turned the bike off and glanced back at her.

Chrissy just sat there, her skin warm and her body humming.

His eyes widened. "Fuck. Don't look at me like that."

She swallowed. "I can't help it."

He lowered his voice. "Your panties wet?"

"None of your business."

"They are," he growled.

They were. And her nipples were hard nubs against her armor.

He leaned closer, his warm breath brushing her cheek. "Well, I can't take you for another bike ride safely outside, but when we get back, I'll let you climb on and ride me."

Her pulse stuttered. She had a clear mental image of him stretched out beneath her, with her riding him hard and taking that big cock deep. She blew out a breath. "I doubt that would be quite as much fun."

His white teeth flashed. "Liar."

"Shovels out," Tane called out. "Let's dig."

Chrissy climbed off the bike, forcing her mind onto the mission. At least her fear had receded. The men took a moment to debate the right spot in the center of the dirt road. Chrissy stayed on the sidelines, watching them work together. They might be rough, but they were a team. She suspected this was a side to the berserkers that most people in the Enclave never saw, or wouldn't even guess existed.

Griff and Dom started digging with the sonic shovels, carving into the hard-packed road. After a few minutes, they swapped with Ash and Levi. She watched the flex of muscles in Levi's arms as he worked.

Instantly, she wanted him again. Her system was fully revved. When she got back to the Enclave, she'd have to see Liberty. The general's partner was the person in charge of the underground market of beauty products, condoms, and apparently vibrators. Chrissy closed her eyes for a second. *God. Focus, Chrissy.*

"Guys, the alien convoy is getting close," Indy said. "Ten minutes. And you have three vehicles incoming."

"Three?" Tane said, his voice unhappy. "It's usually two. Why the change?"

"I don't know, boss-man."

"Any sign they know we're here?"

"Not that I can detect."

Tane nodded at the rectangular hole they were digging. "Speed it up. We'll have company soon."

The men finished digging the hole. It was narrow, running along the road, and only a couple of meters long. It was just deep enough for three people to sit in. It reminded Chrissy of the old mechanic pit back at her father's garage.

"Ash?" Tane said.

Ash unraveled a brown mesh net. He set it over the hole, and Griff and Dom covered it in a layer of dirt.

Chrissy stepped back and studied it. It was barely distinguishable from the rest of the road.

Ash peeled the edge back and Levi dropped into the hole. He crouched down, resting his carbine on the ground, and looked up at her. "You're next."

She stepped in and dropped down beside him. It was a tight fit, and she was pressed up against his body. A second later, Hemi joined them, and Chrissy found herself squished in between two sets of broad shoulders. Now, it was a very tight fit.

Tane crouched by the edge. "We'll get an alien vehicle to stop above you. Then it's up to you to get it disabled."

Chrissy nodded. *No pressure.*

"Once they abandon it, we'll lead them away. In that time, you get the trike operational, and back to the Enclave."

She released a breath. God, she hoped this worked.

"Good luck," Ash said.

"Take care of my bike, Connors," Levi said. "Or you'll answer to me."

Ash smiled. "I'll take good care of her." With a wink, he laid the net back down.

And then it was just the three of them, trapped in the dappled darkness. *Waiting*. She listened to the crunch of boots on dirt as the other berserkers left.

"So, you guys are getting naked, huh?" Hemi asked.

Levi snorted. "You're the biggest gossip in the Enclave, Rahia."

"That's not an answer," Hemi said.

"Yes," Levi said.

"No," Chrissy said.

Hemi grinned and leaned against the dirt wall, his carbine resting across his legs. "It's like that, is it?"

"It was one time." Chrissy refused to look at either one of them, instead looking up through the dirt and net above. How far away were the aliens?

"It's going to happen again," Levi said. "A lot."

She whipped her head around to meet his gaze, and saw the determined glint in his eye.

Shit. She was in trouble.

She was about to open her mouth and blast him, when she heard the rumble of engines. The noise echoed through the quiet above, and there was a rush of flapping wings as some birds took flight from a nearby tree. Her belly went tight.

The engine noise got louder. The aliens were getting close now. Her heartbeat echoed in her head like a drum.

All of a sudden, something exploded with a roar of noise. The ground shook, and a fine mist of dirt rained down on them.

Hemi grinned, his teeth white in the gloom. "Showtime."

CHAPTER NINE

T he air in their little hole in the ground was tense as they waited. Levi gripped his carbine as he listened to weapons fire above—carbines and the distinctive sound of the alien weapons.

Beside him, he felt the tension pumping off Chrissy. He was used to these kinds of situations. He knew to stay relaxed in the tensest moments, and conserve his energy for when he needed it.

Suddenly, they were plunged into darkness. He looked up. A vehicle crawled slowly over them. Levi counted in his head, willing the trike to stop.

But it kept moving and dappled light appeared again. *Come on, Tane.*

There was another boom, closer this time, and more dirt rained down. Levi heard Chrissy gasp, and then her hand gripped his. He tangled their fingers together and squeezed.

Another vehicle rolled slowly over the top of their hiding place. It was firing, making the ground vibrate.

Come on, you bastards. Stop.

The vehicle shuddered, probably hit by one of the guys' grenades. It slowed for a second, but it didn't stop.

Hemi muttered a curse.

"One more," Chrissy murmured.

The third vehicle rolled over them, and Levi's pulse spiked. *Come on.*

Another barrage of weapons fire. Then *boom*.

"Grenade," Hemi said.

The alien vehicle slowed. Levi sensed Chrissy holding her breath, and his hand clenched on his carbine.

The trike stopped.

Yes. "You're up, Spitfire." Levi nudged the net cover aside and helped her up.

The three of them popped up under the alien vehicle. The sharp stench of smoke mixed with alien poison filled the air. He stared at the ink-black underside of the trike. Every now and then, lines of glowing red lights pulsed along the underbody.

"I'll keep watch," Hemi said, his voice low. "Do your thing, because we won't have long."

Chrissy pointed to a panel on the belly of the trike. "I need to get in there."

She squeezed closer to Levi, reaching up with her electro-driver. The tool whizzed quietly, and she worked steadily until the metal panel fell off. A red gush of warm liquid followed, drenching both of them.

"Ugh." She wiped her hand across her face. Levi

leaned over and spat the gross-tasting stuff out of his mouth.

Heedless of the gunk coating her, Chrissy continued on, focused on her task. Levi found himself watching her face, his gaze sliding over the perfect slope of her nose.

He gripped his carbine harder and blew out a breath. He'd never been attracted to a woman because of her damn nose before. What the hell was wrong with him?

But he knew true, real beauty when he saw it. And he didn't just mean what she looked like.

"Come on, you alien piece of shit," she muttered, trying to loosen something. She pushed hard, her arms straining.

"Here." He set his carbine down and wrapped his arms around her. He gripped her hands and they pushed together.

A second later, a second panel fell open, and a small tangle of alien cables fell out.

"Thanks." She snatched up the laser cutter.

One cable started undulating gently, heading for Chrissy's hand.

"Not this time." Levi gripped the cable. "Do it."

She reached out and quickly cut the cable. Above, the trike's engine stopped.

"Nice job, Spitfire." He grinned at her and she grinned back.

Then he heard doors open, and the deep grunts of the raptor language.

Shit. "Back down," Levi bit out.

"I need to get the panel back on, or they'll know

something's wrong." Chrissy leaned up higher, one knee pressed against the edge of the hole.

"Hurry."

"I am," she snapped.

Levi watched as a pair of giant raptor boots came into view, exactly level with them. "Chrissy," he hissed.

She set the panel back into place. "There." She dropped back down into the hole, and Levi quickly pulled the net back in place.

Hemi had already ducked low, and they sat there, huddled together, waiting for shouts or weapons fire. Instead, there were more grunts, and doors slamming.

He heard a big body slither under the vehicle. Dirt trickled down into their hideout. Chrissy's hand landed on his thigh, her fingers digging into his armor.

The raptor above them grunted. *Fuck.* If the bastard moved a few more centimeters, he'd land in their hole.

There was another boom. Levi knew it was a missile from the launcher on his bike. It sounded farther away. In the distance, carbine fire sounded.

The raptor above them moved again with a grunt and a slide of dirt.

"Levi? Hemi?" Tane's voice. "The raptors are abandoning the vehicle to give chase."

"Hell, yeah," Levi murmured, bumping his shoulder against a grinning Chrissy.

"Stay down for now," Indy said, in their earpieces. "I've confirmed that there are no additional raptors in the trike, and I'll let you know when they are far enough away for you to come out."

"Tane and the others will lead them on a merry chase," Hemi said.

More minutes ticked by, and the sound of weapons fire petered out. Then Indy was back. "You're clear."

"Get that damn vehicle operational," Tane growled on the comm.

Levi touched his earpiece. "We're on it."

They climbed out of the hole, shimmying on their bellies to get out from under the alien vehicle.

Hemi stood. "I'm on watch. I'll circle the area. Levi, you keep an eye on Chrissy while she works. And not just on her mighty fine ass."

Chrissy rolled her eyes and Levi scowled at his friend. "You have a woman, keep your eyes off mine."

"Yours?" Chrissy spluttered.

Hemi's grin widened. "My woman has a fine ass too."

Levi grinned back. "I'm telling her you said that." Cam would probably give Hemi a black eye.

Ignoring them, Chrissy dropped down and wiggled back under the vehicle. "While you two act like idiots, I'm going to get this vehicle working again."

Hemi headed off with a wave, and Levi watched Chrissy's boots as she worked on fixing the cables she'd cut. He yanked his water bottle off his belt, and washed out his mouth and splashed his face. He could still taste that damned red raptor gunk.

A few minutes passed, and she slid out. She stood, dusting herself off. "Right, let's get it open."

He held out the water bottle. "You have dried raptor gunk on your face."

Her nose wrinkled, and she took the bottle and

quickly washed her face. Then, she turned back to the vehicle. The trike had a door on each side and a cargo door at the back. Chrissy gripped a handle on the side door and tried to open it. She shook her head.

Then she pulled out her laser cutter and smiled. Seconds later, she pried the door of the alien vehicle open.

A horrible smell wafted out.

"Jesus." Levi grimaced. It smelled like rotting meat.

"Gross," Chrissy muttered.

Inside, there were large, semi-reclined seats big enough for raptor bodies. Cables dangled from the roof, and everything was a standard Gizzida mix of tech and organic. Metal and bone. Composites and sinew.

Hemi reappeared. "I'll ride in the back."

Levi nodded. "Only two seats in the front here, anyway."

"I have to work out how to drive it first." With her nose wrinkled, Chrissy slid into the driver's seat. "I know some of the parts for these things, but I don't know the controls for driving."

Levi leaned in. "Can you do it?"

She gave him a grim, determined smile. "I'll do it."

CHRISSY TOUCHED the spongy controls and pulled bone-like levers. Red lights flared on, but the vehicle wasn't moving.

She blew out a breath, and reached into a recess on

the console filled with alien cables. She pulled them apart, and hated when they moved against her hand.

Nothing was working.

Outside, Levi and Hemi were keeping watch, their carbines resting in their arms. But she could tell both men were tense. They were running out of time.

She touched some more things—they might be buttons. Nothing. Maybe it was coded for raptor DNA, or something.

Dammit. She slammed her palms on the console and suddenly lights flared to life.

Excitement made her straighten, but then she watched the lights die out. She cursed bitterly, the worst ones she'd picked up from her dad when he thought no one was listening.

"Babe." Levi leaned in, one tattooed arm resting along the door frame. He looked amused.

"Don't 'babe' me, biker man."

"Babe," he said again. "You can finesse a Hunter engine in your sleep. I've seen some of the sweet little upgrades you've added to the Hunters. You can sort out this alien piece of crap."

His easy confidence in her skills made her chest expand. Her dad's praise had always been grudging and part surprised.

"Don't be nice to me, King."

He winked at her. "I can be very nice if you'll let me."

Trying to ignore his blatant sexiness, she blew an escaped strand of hair out of her face, and pulled open a panel on the console. She stared at the red, jelly-like goop inside. Boy, that smelled bad. Like days-old fish in the warm sun.

Gritting her teeth, she reached her gloved hand into the viscous substance and almost gagged at the smell. Her hand closed around what felt like a small balloon.

What the hell? Cautiously, she squeezed the balloon. The engine started.

"Woo-hoo!" Levi leaned in again. "Nice work, Spitfire."

She touched the bone levers. "Step back. Now I need to work out how to get this thing moving."

Pulling the first lever, the vehicle lurched forward. *Whoa.* Okay, forward. She touched another, and the trike turned to the left, moving forward with a throaty growl. She got a few meters when the engine cut out.

"Levi, Hemi, and Chrissy?" Indy's voice again. "You need to go. There's another raptor patrol incoming. Looks like they're the backup for the team chasing the rest of the squad. You need to move. *Now*."

The other door opened and Levi slid into the passenger seat. "You're out of time. We've got to go."

"Levi, so far we can move forward a bit and turn left!"

"It'll have to do. Work the rest out en route to the Enclave."

Gritting her teeth, she got the engine started again. She heard a fist thump against the back with a dull echo, and realized Hemi was aboard.

Now or never. Letting out a slow, controlled breath, she touched the levers again, and they rolled forward.

She did a wide left turn, bumping over road and grass, before she got them back on the road.

"There you go," Levi said.

She touched more controls, working out the right turn and increasing their speed. They rolled down the road, moving faster. At the next corner, she misjudged, and they bumped off the dirt and onto the grass.

"Tree coming up," Levi called out.

"Don't backseat drive," she grumbled, correcting her steering.

Back on the road, Chrissy fought to keep the vehicle straight. They needed to get back to the Enclave, so she decided to risk more speed. Soon the trees on either side of the road became a blur.

Then, the trike hit some loose gravel.

The vehicle fishtailed, and Chrissy bit down on her lip. She wrenched on the controls. *Don't flip. Don't flip.*

She gripped the brake lever, and they came to a hard stop. Levi flew forward, slapping his hand against the console to stop himself from smashing into it.

"Sorry," she cried out.

"Keep driving, Spitfire."

Gripping the controls, every muscle in her body tight, she focused on driving and keeping them on the road.

Soon, they turned off the dirt road onto a paved one. It was deteriorating in patches, but flat enough for her to accelerate more. It still wasn't the smoothest ride, but now they were covering some ground.

"We see you coming," Indy said.

Chrissy sent up a silent prayer. *Thank you, God.* Her

shoulders, arms, and hands were so tight they were hurting.

She looked ahead and recognized the green valley. It was hard to imagine that the lush farmland hid a huge underground base built in a former coal mine. She turned onto the grass, bumping over a collapsed fence. She knew that there was a hidden ramp that base security would open up for them.

"A little more to the south, Chrissy," Indy instructed.

Suddenly, the engine died.

"No. No." Chrissy thumped the console. She tried to get the engine started but got nothing.

"Chrissy..."

"I'm trying," she snapped at him. Then she threw her door open.

"Chrissy!"

She dropped down and slid under the vehicle. The panel she'd messed was hanging open, cables dangling out. *Shit.*

Stuffing them back in, she saw one cable was glowing red and damaged. Jaw locking, she pulled out her laser cutter. She didn't have any spare alien parts or enough knowledge on their systems, so she'd have to wing it.

With a quick slice, she cut the cable, ignoring as it waved around. She cut out the damaged part and pressed it back together. She retracted her helmet and snatched the band out of her hair. She reached up, wrapping the tie around the cable. Damn, it wasn't enough to hold it.

She turned and saw Levi crouched, watching her.

"I need your hair band."

He raised a brow, but retracted his helmet and pulled

out his man bun. As he handed the elastic to her, she eyed his shoulder-length strands of dirty blonde hair. He looked good with his hair out.

Looking up, she used the band to hold the cable together and slammed the panel closed. Moments later, she was back in the trike. It fired up first time.

They resumed bouncing across the field.

"Pretty handy with some elastic," he murmured.

"Sometimes you just have to make do."

Levi leaned forward and pointed. "There."

Chrissy spotted the hole opening up in the ground. She slowed the trike, and drove straight down into darkness. Lights automatically flicked on along the side walls of the ramp. They descended straight down before turning in a spiral and flattening out. Moments later, she saw a square of light ahead, and they drove into the Hunter hangar.

She pulled the trike to a stop and dropped her head forward. *They'd made it.* She flexed her aching hands.

Levi reached over, his gloved hand gripping the back of her neck. He squeezed. "Nice job, Spitfire."

She looked straight into his sexy eyes. All the stress and strain of the mission churned in her, and found a target. Rough, hard sex with Levi was just what the doctor ordered. She deserved some orgasms, dammit.

She was about to say something when their doors opened. She turned her head and saw Holmes, Niko, and Indy waiting for them. Hemi joined them, swinging his carbine onto his back.

"Well done," Holmes said.

"Thanks," Chrissy said.

"Tane and the others are on their way back," Indy said with a smile, her ink-black ponytail swinging behind her. Her bold gaze ran along the alien vehicle. "Nice work."

"Holy shit." John, Bec, and several of the other maintenance mechanics rushed over.

"She in full working order?" a man named Luke asked.

"Sure is." Chrissy climbed out of the trike.

The crew started peppering her with questions.

Chrissy held up a hand. "Hey, guys, I smell bad, and I have an impending adrenaline crash due. I think I'll at least shower before I do anything with her."

She shrugged away the fib. She wasn't really feeling like she was going to crash. She felt pumped. She couldn't believe she'd actually done it! She'd stolen an alien vehicle.

"Go clean up and get some rest, Chrissy," Holmes said. "You've earned it. And thank you."

She pointed to her fellow mechanics. "Don't break it while I'm gone."

Hemi wrapped his arms around her in a bear hug, lifting her off her feet. "You did a fucking good job out there, Red."

"Thanks."

When he set her down, she headed for the door. Levi fell into step with her.

"You were awesome out there," he said. "It was really good work."

She glanced his way. "You too."

Hot tension stirred between them, making her skin

prickle. Her brain was screaming at her to stay the hell away from this man, but her lady parts were saying something very different.

As soon as they stepped out of the hangar and into the empty corridor, Levi grabbed her. In a split second, Chrissy found herself backed up against the wall.

She didn't stop to think. Throwing her arms around his hard body, she leaned up, meeting him halfway.

His tongue swept into her mouth, his hands slamming into the wall beside her body. She sucked on his tongue and he groaned.

Then he was kissing her. It was hard, rough, and unapologetic.

She hated that they were both still in their armor. She wanted skin, and heat, and Levi.

And, throwing caution to the wind, she decided she was going to take him. She'd been the good girl all her life and look where it had gotten her. Now, it was time to be bad.

CHAPTER TEN

White-hot need thundered through Levi. He liked to fuck when he got back from a mission, high on adrenaline, and filled with the need to celebrate still being alive.

But for the first time ever, his lust was focused on one particular woman.

"I want you." His voice was guttural.

He bit down on her lush bottom lip and she moaned.

He dragged his mouth down the side of her neck, sucking the salt off her skin. He raked his teeth over the tendon in her neck and she moved against him.

"I want to be buried deep inside you." His voice was a husky growl. "I want you to scream my name when you come this time."

Her hands slid into his hair, tugging. She writhed that sexy body against him. "Whose room is closer?"

Elation tore through him. "Mine." He scooped her up

into his arms and she wrapped her legs around his waist. "I'm so fucking hard." He groaned.

"Hurry."

He moved fast, ignoring everyone they passed. Chrissy kept tormenting him, her lips nipping at his ear.

When he reached his door, he slammed his hand to the lock. She was kissing his neck and his cock was in agony, trapped behind his armor.

They needed to shower first. And he had to say, the idea of being in the shower with a naked Chrissy and water running over both of them was one he liked. A hell of a lot.

He stepped inside and came to a halt.

"What the hell?" he barked.

In his arms, Chrissy tensed and lifted her head to look over her shoulder. She tensed even more.

There was a naked woman in the center of his bed.

"Hey." The woman smiled under a cloud of teased brown hair. "Surprise." She ran her hand down her flat belly, heading toward her bare mound.

Chrissy struggled to be let down, but Levi kept hold of her. He stared at the woman, thinking that she looked vaguely familiar. Maybe he'd partied with her before? Chrissy squirmed again.

"How the fuck did you get in here?" he said.

The brunette stilled, clearly picking up on his mood. "I like to party." Gamely, she flicked her gaze to Chrissy. "You want a threesome? I could get into that."

A strangled sound escaped Chrissy, her cheeks suffused with hot color. "Put me down."

"Chrissy—"

"Let me go," she hissed.

Fuck. Levi set her on her feet.

"I'm an idiot," she muttered, spinning toward the door.

He reached for her, his gut tightening. "Chrissy—"

"No." She held up a hand. "Don't touch me." She backed toward the door. "Just...just forget it. I should have known better." She flicked a look at the woman. "Enjoy your night." She charged out the door.

"Fuck!" Levi turned and kicked the wall. His boot sank into the plaster, leaving a gaping hole.

The woman on his bed sat up, clutching a silky shirt to her chest. "Ah, this didn't go how I planned."

"Get out."

The woman scrambled up, yanking on her clothes. "I...I'm sorry. I didn't mean anything, I was just after a good time."

"Then you should have asked." Levi shoved a hand through his hair. "How'd you get in?"

She shrugged a shoulder. "There's a guy on the tech team..."

Who she'd charmed. She shot Levi a cautious smile and slipped out.

Shit. There was only one woman Levi wanted, and right now, if he got anywhere near her, she'd kick, claw, or punch him. Or skewer him with her electro-driver.

He tore off his upper armor and tossed it. It bounced off the wall.

He stomped over to his kitchenette. The cupboards were all empty, except for one. He grabbed a bottle of bourbon and twisted the top off.

Snatching a glass from the sink—he was pretty sure it was clean—he dropped down into a chair and poured a healthy slug into the glass. He picked it up and knocked it back.

Chrissy hadn't even given him a fucking chance. He knew he had a reputation, one he didn't give a shit about. He lived life his own way. But they'd just survived a dangerous mission, and *dammit*, they'd worked well together.

He poured another two fingers of bourbon. He was going to sit here and get drunk, because Levi King had never chased a woman. Never.

He knocked back the bourbon, savoring the burn.

Then he slammed the glass down on the table. Fuck that. Chrissy Hagan was *his*. He was claiming that delicious ass of hers all for himself.

Standing, he stripped the rest of his armor and his clothes off. First, he needed a shower, and then he was going to stake his claim. With his cock lodged deep inside her and her body shaking from multiple orgasms, she'd know just who she belonged to.

CHRISSY SLICED THROUGH THE WATER. She'd lost count of how many laps she'd done in the Enclave swimming pool.

Since she'd first arrived here, bruised and battered, the gorgeous underground pool had delighted her. She swum laps a few times a week and ordinarily it soothed her.

Not tonight.

She stopped at the end and leaned her head against the cool tiles. It was really late, so she had the place to herself. That, she was grateful for.

She didn't need any witnesses to her misery. *Dammit to hell.* For a second there—

No. She wasn't thinking about Levi. She wasn't becoming a member of his parade of lovers.

Turning, she pushed off into the water. As she did more laps, her anger didn't go away. His encouragement out on the mission had meant a lot to her, not to mention the way he'd looked out for her.

Swimming harder, she decided she needed to be so tired that she'd fall asleep without even thinking about him. When she reached the end of the lap, she paused, chest heaving. When she lifted her head, a pair of boots and jeans stood at the side of the pool and she froze.

She looked up.

Damn him for looking so good and so sexy. He'd showered, and for once, he'd left his tawny hair loose. It brushed his broad shoulders.

"That was quick." She knew he couldn't miss the acid in her voice.

"I didn't fuck her," he growled. "She came uninvited. Apparently she conned one of the tech geeks to let her in. I got rid of her two seconds after you ran out."

"You should have taken her up on her offer."

"Get out of the pool, Chrissy."

"I do whatever the hell I want, biker man." She lifted her chin. "That no longer includes you."

Levi reached down and gripped both her wrists. In

one move, he pulled her up and out of the pool. Her heart thumped against her chest at the display of strength. Then her feet touched the edge of the pool and she was facing him, water streaming off her.

He yanked her against him. "Nice bikini, Spitfire."

It was tiny and black. She felt water soaking into his worn T-shirt and jeans.

"You're getting wet." She tried to pull away.

"I don't care." He sank a hand into her sopping hair, tugging her head back. "I don't want anyone else. I want you. I would have explained that back in my room if you'd given me a chance."

Chrissy felt the sting of his words. Damn, she had run off like some pent-up schoolgirl.

"Watching you today, how fucking brave you were. How damn good you are at your work..."

Now her chest hitched, and she felt something inside her tremble.

"You're the entire package, Chrissy. Beautiful, fresh, good, kind, smart, brave."

Her heart squeezed.

Levi leaned down. "I never get beauty. Not the real, deep kind." His nose ran down her cheek. "Now I've tasted it, I want more."

This was all too much. Swallowing against the lump in her throat, she tried not to lose herself. Somehow, this man reached down and touched things inside her. Things that had been shriveled and nearly dead for a long time. Her head was still warning her that this sexy biker man, who did whatever the hell he wanted, whenever he wanted it, wasn't really a good bet.

She pushed against his chest. She had to get away from him. She knew that sex with Levi was mind blowing, but he was dangerous to her.

"Not letting you go." His hands tightened on her. "I want you and you want me."

Oh, God. "I'll make you a deal," she said, desperation filling her.

He raised a brow. "I'm listening."

"Just sex."

Both his brows went up. "Say again."

"Let's have at this until it burns out," she said matter-of-factly.

Because it would. Because he'd find some pretty, young thing that caught his interest eventually, and he'd move on. She'd try, but never make him happy. Her entire life, she'd bent over backwards for the people in her life—her father, her sister—and it had never been enough.

What Chrissy didn't need was a broken heart on top of trying to survive a damn alien apocalypse.

"Let's get this out of our system," she said boldly.

She saw something harden in Levi's eyes. "You just want to fuck, sweet thing? All right, then let's fuck."

When he reached for her, she held her hand up. "I say when and where."

Ignoring her, he snatched her off her feet and planted a hard kiss on her lips. "We'll see."

On instinct, she wrapped her legs around his waist, and instantly felt a hard, denim-covered bulge brush between her legs. She bit back a moan.

A second later, he had her bikini top off.

"Damn, these are pretty." He lifted her up, his mouth latching onto one breast.

Oh, God. Her head fell back and she moaned in pleasure. "Someone...might come in—"

"I locked the door behind me." He sucked her nipple into his mouth, licking hard.

God, so much sensation. She rolled her hips against him.

He switched to her other breast, his goatee rasping against her skin. Desire was washing over her like a wave.

"Gonna fuck you hard, Spitfire. So hard you'll be screaming."

She felt the control slipping through her fingers. Maybe this hadn't been her best idea, after all.

Then he was moving, striding away from the edge of the pool. He spun her around, lowering her onto the long, low bench where she'd left her towel.

He set her down on all fours.

She gripped the edge of the bench. "Levi—"

"Don't move. Ass in the air, Spitfire." His fingers toyed with the ties on the side of her bikini bottoms.

A millisecond later, the bottoms were gone with a tug, and Chrissy was naked. She felt a rough hand run over her ass, kneading the flesh.

"Best ass I've ever seen, Chrissy." He delved between her thighs. "And the hottest, tightest pussy."

God, what did he have planned? She trembled. He plunged two fingers inside her, and she rocked back against him. *So good.*

"Soaked. All just for me."

She felt him move behind her, and then she felt his lips and beard scrape her thighs. She quivered.

"Hold on tight, Spitfire. You're going to need to."

Chrissy suddenly felt like she'd made a deal with the devil. She just hoped she survived it. Survived him.

Then his mouth was on her, licking and sucking. His hands gripped her thighs, pulling her back on his face. He groaned, a rough sound of pleasure, and it vibrated through her. Then his tongue plunged inside her.

She arched her back. *Oh, God.*

CHAPTER ELEVEN

D amn, she tasted like the sweetest honey. Levi licked Chrissy's folds, then stabbed his tongue inside her. He could eat her all day long, for every meal. And the little, hungry sounds escaping her were driving him wild.

She pushed back against his mouth, wanting more.

Using his lips, tongue, and teeth, he pushed her to the edge. Then he growled against her clit before he sucked it into his mouth.

Suddenly, her body stiffened and she screamed as she came, her legs shaking around his face.

Need was like a relentless one-two punch to his gut. His pulse pounding, he rose up behind her, straddling the bench. He opened his jeans and freed his cock.

He rubbed the swollen head of his cock through her slick folds. Damn, that was a pretty view. His cock looked far too big to fit inside that sweet body.

"Beg me for it," he growled.

"No way." Her voice was husky. "Just *do* it." She looked over her shoulder. Her eyes were glazed, but blazing with challenge. She rubbed against him, his cock notching at her entrance.

HE COULDN'T WAIT another second. He *needed* to be inside her. He pushed forward, and with a single thrust, he filled her to the hilt.

She moaned, a hot, hungry sound.

Levi gripped her hips, and then started slamming into her. She pushed back against him, meeting every thrust. Damn, that ass and those curves were perfection.

He sped up, until the only sound echoing through the room was of flesh slapping flesh. He felt his orgasm tightening inside him, but he gritted his teeth. He was going to make her come again first.

For the first time in his life, he wished he could see his lover's face as he fucked her. Next time, he wasn't fucking her from behind.

"I want you to come again, Spitfire."

She just moaned.

Levi slid one hand under her and found her clit. He rolled the swollen nub between his fingers.

"Yes," she cried.

He felt her body tensing and he leaned over her. He pressed his mouth to her ear.

"Say my name this time, Chrissy. Otherwise, I'll keep fucking you right here until you do." He slowed down, dragging his cock out of her.

"Be quiet," she pleaded. "Just keep moving."

He slid inside her slowly, and pulled out. He gave her clit another squeeze. "I'll make this slow and long. And if you don't say my name, next up, I'll fuck that pretty face of yours, and then eat you again. Then I'll make you ride me..."

She moved against him. "That's...not much of a deterrent."

When he pulled out of her again, she made a frustrated cry.

She looked back at him. "Levi."

Yes. He couldn't hold back anymore. He gripped her hips hard, and resumed thrusting inside her. Damn, she was perfect—beauty and sweet, mixed with hot and dirty.

When he rolled her clit again, she came.

"Levi!" Her body clamped down on his cock.

And the sound of his name on her lips drove him over the edge.

He slammed into her, over and over, until he filled her, holding himself deep. He wrapped an arm around her chest, yanking her back against him. Her head hit his shoulder, and his roar joined her cries, as he poured himself inside her.

AS LEVI PULLED out of her, Chrissy bit her lip to keep from crying out.

Everything was too much. Levi was too much, and all the feelings inside her were too much. She felt like he'd stripped everything away and left her bare and out of control.

She turned and sprawled on the bench. God, her legs felt like jelly. She wondered if she could even stand.

Levi sat there, legs straddling the bench, his cock still free. She licked her lips. He hadn't really softened that much.

"Like what you see, Spitfire?" A satisfied drawl.

Chrissy felt her belly quiver. *Sex. Just sex, remember.* She wanted some control back, and she wanted to drive that smug look off his face.

She moved back up on her hands and knees, crawling toward him.

He cocked a brow. "Feeling hungry?" He leaned back.

She stopped between his legs, pressing a hand to his hard thigh. "I want that big cock in my mouth. I'm planning to show you how hard I can make you come."

His muscles tensed. "I just emptied myself in your tight pussy, Chrissy. I know."

"You haven't seen anything yet, biker man."

His breath hitched. "Fuck."

She palmed his cock and a groan vibrated through him. Power trickled through her. Oh, yeah, she liked having him under her, eager and hungry. She looked into his hooded eyes, then lowered her head.

Chrissy licked the pre-come off the tip, then dragged her tongue down his long length. She traced a thick vein, then followed it back up. She opened her mouth and wrapped her lips around his cock.

"Goddamn." Levi's hips jerked up.

She sucked harder, taking him deeper. His tortured groans spurred her on, and she felt a rush of dampness between her thighs. She looked at his face and saw his gaze locked on her lips. Pulling off, she licked around his swollen head, finding a sensitive spot that made him curse. With a smile, she slipped her mouth over him again.

Oh, yes, she loved having Levi King at her mercy.

His fingers slipped into her hair, but he didn't try to take over. He tugged on her hair, hard enough to have a pleasurable sting shoot across her scalp. She moaned.

"I'm going to come soon, Spitfire."

She sucked harder, her cheeks going hollow.

Another curse and this time he angled her head so more of his cock slipped into her mouth. His hips bumped up and then he grabbed her under her arms and yanked her up onto his chest.

She was about to protest, when he spun her, and she found herself facing that big cock again. She circled her fingers around him, just as he spread her thighs with his hands and his mouth landed between her legs.

Chrissy cried out. *No.* She wasn't coming again before he did.

She sucked his cock deep into her mouth, bobbing her head. He lapped at her, using his teeth and tongue.

Oh, God, she was going to come. She tightened her belly, trying to hold back. She sucked harder, locked in this sexy battle.

"Fuck, Chrissy." His hips bumped up and she felt him spurt in her mouth as he came. She swallowed as fast as she could and a millisecond later, her own orgasm rocketed through her. Lights burst in front of her eyes.

Levi's cock slid from her mouth and she threw her

head back. "Levi."

She collapsed against him, air sawing in and out of her lungs. He was breathing heavily too, and she smiled.

"Damn, you know how to wreck a man." A big hand palmed her ass. "I will not forget that anytime soon."

Little waves of pleasure still shivered through her. All the chaotic emotions raced back in. He kept stroking her and she told herself to just enjoy it. Fun and orgasms.

But instead of feeling in control, she felt like she was on some wild rollercoaster...and the only way off was to jump.

She moved quickly, standing up and grabbing her towel. She wrapped it around her naked body.

"Where are you going?"

She tried to keep her face blank as she looked up at him. He was watching her with narrowed eyes. *Just sex, Chrissy. You can do this.*

"I have work to do. My guys took some control parts off the trike that we can't figure out. I'm going to take them back to my room and work on them. I need to get a better understanding of what makes that vehicle tick, before we risk taking it out into the field." Especially underwater, in the heart of alien territory.

His mouth pressed into a line. "Just like that?" He straightened, tucking that magnificent cock back into his jeans. "My come is still dripping down your thighs and you're rushing off?"

God, that dirty mouth of his. She pressed the aforementioned—and sticky—thighs together. "I'm pretty sure you've fucked a lot of women, biker man. I thought you'd be used to this."

He lifted his chin. "Yeah, used to them being hot for the next round and clinging for more."

"Well, I'm not clinging."

She saw something dark cross his face.

"Wham-bam, and you're done, is it?" His voice was gritty.

She rolled her eyes. "You've wham-bammed half the Enclave, Levi. What do you care?"

He scowled at her.

Chrissy pushed her hopelessly tangled hair back. She needed to get out of there, and get away from him. Maybe without him and his biker badass sexiness in her face, she could think straight. "I've got better things to do."

Levi straightened, his expression turning as hard as a rock. "Better things. Right."

Chrissy stilled. She couldn't quite read his face, but her words seem to have struck deep. There was something pained buried in his eyes, and she didn't like it. "Levi—"

"You got your fucking orgasm, so go." He turned away, grabbing his shirt and thrusting his arms through it. "I need a fucking drink."

The harsh tone of his voice made her belly clench. "Levi—"

He turned, his gaze moving right through her. "Forget it. Come find me if you need another fuck."

He strode out of the pool room with that loose-hipped stride of his, and Chrissy stood there, not exactly sure what had happened.

She didn't know what she'd done, but she knew it wasn't good.

CHAPTER TWELVE

L evi stormed into the rec room. He scanned the space and spotted Griff, Dom, and Manu sitting in some chairs on the far side of the room. Manu was big and hard to miss.

Stopping at the bar, Levi grabbed a bottle of bourbon and poured himself a glass. Most of the alcohol these days was homebrewed, but the Enclave still had a pretty decent stock of the good stuff.

When he dropped into a chair with the guys, he felt them all looking at him.

"Rough night?" Griff asked.

Levi sank back and lifted his glass. "Something like that. Women."

Manu let out a booming laugh. "Women. Can't live with them, can't live without them."

Taking a large sip of his drink, Levi savored the burn. *I've got better things to do.* Chrissy's words kept repeating in his head, but they kept morphing into a deeper, harsher tone. His father's voice.

I got better things to do. You're good for nothing, boy.

He took another sip.

"A good woman is worth some bumps in the road," Dom said quietly.

"How would you know?" Griff said. "You don't have a woman."

When Dom just raised one dark brow, Levi wondered if the man was holding out on them. If anyone could keep a secret, it was Dom Santora.

Manu lifted his beer. "Are you sure your woman isn't off having a similar conversation about you being an asshole?"

Levi shrugged. "She thinks I'm an asshole even when she likes me." He remembered the confused look on her face as he'd left the pool room. Shit, he'd overreacted to her words.

He closed his eyes and took another sip of his drink. He knew she hadn't meant anything by it. She wanted to work on the alien parts to help the mission. Still, she didn't need to go from hot and sweet, to racing off like he was something she needed to scrape off her shoe.

He blew out a breath. "I'm feeling better already." He stretched his legs out, crossing them at the ankles. His friends were all smiling at him...at his expense. "What, none of you ever have woman trouble?"

"I stay clear," Griff said. "Had a woman once. Was engaged to her. As soon as I went to prison, she walked, even when I told her I wasn't guilty. She didn't trust me, and she sure as hell didn't know me." Griff stared intently at his glass. "She was supposed to love me and have my back."

Levi stared at the tiny bit of amber liquid left in his glass. Chrissy was fierce when she was protecting something she cared about. If she was his, she'd have his back, no matter what.

He straightened, ice clinking in his glass. *His?* Shit. Except for his disastrous, short-lived marriage, he'd never tied himself to a woman. Hadn't thought he'd want to again.

"What about you, Dom?" he asked.

The dark-haired man shrugged his shoulders. "My previous...employment was dangerous work. Women didn't hang around long, and the ones that did weren't the ones I wanted."

Levi read between the lines. When you worked for the Mafia, it was hard to meet the right woman. And when you were dangerous and intense, and scared men, not just women, it made it even harder.

"I want class, beauty, and grace," Dom said. "It's a hard combination to find."

Levi got that. For the first time in his life, he really got that. Chrissy was his kind of beauty—sexy, sassy, confident.

He glanced at Manu. "Manu? You got any more advice?"

"Bide your time, my friend. Get the lay of the land, evaluate, and have all the info you need before you make your move."

Levi snorted. "I'm not planning to go to war."

Manu sipped his beer. "Love is war, Levi."

Levi didn't know the first thing about love, but he knew that he needed to see Chrissy.

There was something hot and explosive between them, and it was sure as hell more than just the sex she wanted to pretend it was. Besides, he owed her an explanation for him storming off.

He studied his empty glass. First, he needed another drink, because he sucked at apologies.

CHRISSY WALKED down the corridor with an armload of alien parts. They'd all been scanned—twice—to make sure they were safe to take out of the hangar. The last thing she needed was for some alien nasty to pop out of one of them and run amok around everyone's personal quarters.

Once she reached her room, she bumped her hip against her door and moved inside. Hurrying over to the table, she dumped the parts. Next, she grabbed her small toolkit and set it down on the table.

She was still feeling a bit ragged from her encounter with Levi. She needed something to smooth out her mood. Grabbing her candles, she lit a few. Yum, her favorites—mango and vanilla.

Sitting down, she felt an ache between her thighs. Where Levi had been. Her belly clenched. The best kind of sore.

Instantly, she was back in the pool room, imagining his mouth between her legs, her back arched as her orgasm hit her. Remembering his cock powering inside her. Or her lips wrapped around him as she used her mouth on him.

Shit. It was too easy to remember the pleasure, and it was also too easy to remember the way his face had changed before he'd left.

She'd...hurt him.

He'd taken care of her on the mission, and shown her glimpses of another side of him. Instead of being honest with him, she'd hidden behind sex and protecting herself.

The fact was, he scared the hell out of her.

She brushed her hair out of her face and shook her head. She picked up her electro-driver. For now, she needed to focus on her work, not sexy bikers. After some sleep, she'd work out what to say to Levi.

Pulling the parts closer, she set to work. She pulled several things apart, marveling at the sinew holding things together, and the tough, bone-like substance the raptors had used. She picked up a small, black box and set it aside. It looked a little like the alien energy cubes the tech team had collected and used, but smaller. It hadn't given off any sort of signature on the scanner, so she didn't think this was a power source.

She pried a small panel open and got some sticky goo on her fingers. She wrinkled her nose. It was gross, but amazing. She tapped her tool on the table and wondered if there was any way she could incorporate some of this into the Hunters' engines. There were some places where the wear and tear issues were huge, and some of this sinew-type stuff could really help with the engine integrity.

Breathing deep, she pulled in the sweet scent of her

candles. She had quite a little collection now. She glanced around her room, once again thankful to have her own space, and not be stuck in a cage.

Suddenly, a red light blinked on the top of the small box.

Curious, she picked it up, holding it up to her eyes. She tried to open it, but there was no obvious way to do it. She frowned. *What do you do?*

As she turned it over, she saw the flames on her candles flicker and enlarge.

What the hell? She dropped the cube and it bounced on the table. When she looked back at her candles, the flames looked fine.

She shook her head. The stress of the mission, followed by multiple orgasms, had clearly left her exhausted.

But instead of heading for bed, she picked up the cube again and grabbed her electro-driver. She tried to pry the edge of the box open.

All of a sudden, the box made a small, harsh beep and started to emit some warmth.

She stilled, staring at it. Then the thing started to heat up in her hand. It also began to glow—yellow slowly turned to orange.

She stood, her belly hardening. *What the hell?*

Something wasn't right.

The glow intensified, changing to bright red, and now the cube was becoming painfully hot. *Shit.* She dropped it and it clattered off the table. She heard it hit the floor on the other side.

She took a step back toward the door. She needed to

tell someone. Maybe Noah, or someone from the tech team.

Chrissy had taken one more step when she heard a roar of sound, followed by a brilliant flash of light.

A wall of heat slammed into her, and then she was flying. A second wave of heat washed over her and she smelled something burning.

Her body crashed into something and then everything went black.

CHAPTER THIRTEEN

L evi sipped his second drink, watching Manu and Griff fighting it out at the pool table.

Suddenly, a massive explosion of noise roared through the rec room, shaking the walls. Levi dropped into a crouch, and saw his friends do the same. He heard glasses fall and shatter, followed by screams.

Fuck.

"What the hell?" Griff yelled, gripping the pool table.

"Explosion," Manu said.

Levi leaped up. "That was *inside* the Enclave." He raced for the door.

People were shouting and screaming.

"Help these people, Manu." Levi tore through the door, Griff and Dom right behind him.

When they broke into the corridor, he smelled smoke. They turned a corner and he saw Marcus sprinting down the hall.

"Stay in your rooms," Marcus yelled at the people peering out of doorways. "Stay calm."

"What happened?" Levi asked.

"Don't know yet," Marcus said in a gritty voice.

"Gizzida?" Griff said.

The head of Hell Squad shook his head. "There's been no breach in security. The explosion was down in the accommodation area."

Accommodation area? Levi frowned, as he, Griff, and Dom fell in behind Marcus. They jogged down the ramp to the lower level.

Ahead, smoke was billowing in the corridor. In the gloom, he spied the compact form of Kate Scott. The woman and her team all had fire extinguishers, and were putting out the last of the flames.

"Need any help?" Marcus yelled.

The woman shook her head, her bluntly cut hair brushing her jaw. "The blaze is under control. Thankfully, the explosion was localized."

Levi scanned the corridor. A twisted metal door lay on the ground, along with the remnants of what looked like a table. Worried people were gathered at the end of the corridor, looking on. Then he took in the now-destroyed room. The wall and door had been blown out, and the contents were now all charred, blackened remains.

"Whose room?" he asked.

Marcus shook his head. "Don't know."

Something tickled along Levi's senses. "Whose room is this?" he called to Kate.

She glanced back with a frown. "Chrissy Hagan, one

of the Hunter mechanics."

Levi felt like he'd had the wind knocked out of him. Like he'd just taken knuckledusters to the gut. He locked the shock down, trying to make sense of the situation.

"Where is she? Was she inside?"

"I don't have time for this—"

"Where is she?" he roared.

Kate's gaze flickered with understanding. "We're searching for her. No one can say if she was here."

Levi pressed his hands to the back of his neck. *No.* She couldn't have been in there. "Saw her about an hour ago. She was coming back here to work on some alien vehicle parts..."

Sympathy washed over Kate's tough face. "There's no sign anyone survived this explosion."

"Levi?" Griff moved up beside him, watching him intently. Dom did the same on the other side.

He knew what they were doing. They'd lock him down if he lost his shit.

"You find a body?" His voice cracked.

Kate cleared her throat. "The blaze was too hot for—"

"Did. You. Find. A. Body."

She flinched at his tone. "No. But there is unlikely to be one." Pity in her eyes. "I'm sorry."

Suddenly, Levi felt lightheaded and pressed a hand to the wall.

He could hear Griff talking, but to Levi, the words were muffled. His gaze went back to the ruined room and he couldn't look away.

Chrissy couldn't be gone. She *couldn't.*

But a mocking voice inside his head laughed. He'd

never gotten to keep anything good in his life. Of course, he couldn't hold onto her. The voice sounded a lot like his father's.

"Levi."

Ash's voice broke through the haze. The one person who'd been there for him all his life. Ash gripped Levi's shoulder and squeezed.

A massive, horrible feeling clawed at Levi like a wild animal. It welled inside him and he threw his head back and let out a vicious, pained roar.

CHRISSY WANDERED DOWN THE CORRIDOR, dazed, her ears ringing.

She wasn't quite sure what had happened. She'd woken up in the corridor with her table on top of her. All she'd known was that she needed to get away.

Frowning, she pressed her hand to her sore head, and winced. Her hands hurt, too. She looked at them, and then her bare feet. Both were burned and blistered.

What happened? She bit her lip. She couldn't think. She couldn't remember. She stumbled roughly into the wall. She wasn't sure which way to go.

Something had exploded. *Max.* She had to get to Max. He'd worry, and she didn't want him to worry.

She rounded a corner, and bumped into a hard body headed in the opposite direction. Big hands steadied her, and she looked up into Hemi's bearded face.

There was naked relief in his dark eyes. "*Fuck.* It is *so* good to see you, sweetheart."

She frowned. "My head hurts."

He wrapped an arm around her pulling her close. "You just rest here. Take it easy."

She leaned into him, looking down at her bare feet again. They were raw and pink, and edged in black soot. She was vaguely aware of Hemi making a call to someone. "I got her. Yeah, she's *alive*."

Chrissy looked at her shirt and her brow wrinkled. There was a hole ripped in the middle of it. She sniffed, and all she could smell was smoke. *Damn*. This was her favorite top.

Memories burst through her head like an explosion of confetti. *Explosion*. An alien part exploding in her room. Everything going black.

Suddenly, there were running footsteps echoing down the corridor. She looked up to see Levi sprinting toward her. Ash was right behind him.

All the aches and pains exploded inside her and a huge sob escaped her. She took two steps toward Levi and then he swept her into his arms.

"Levi—"

"Fuck. *Fuck*." His arms were tight around her.

"One of the parts blew up—"

"I thought you were dead, Spitfire." He pulled her as close as possible and buried his face in her hair.

"I'm sorry," she murmured. God, his big body was shaking. "I was confused when I came to." He leaned her back, gently probing her head.

"You got a knot back here." His gaze dropped down. "Shit, babe, your hands are burned."

"And my feet." She winced. "And I'm starting to

feel it."

"We need to get you to the infirmary. Now." He glanced at Hemi. "Thanks, man."

"Don't mention it. Go look after your girl."

Levi swept Chrissy off her feet, carrying her like she was a precious bundle.

"You okay, Levi?" Ash asked.

"Yeah. Yeah, I am now. Thanks, Ash."

"Go. I'll catch you both later." He bumped his shoulder against Levi's. "Looks like you are going down, bro." Ash's voice was ripe with amusement. "And I am happy to see it."

"Fuck off, Connors."

Chrissy was too tired and sore to process what they were talking about. As Levi strode down the hall, she let her eyes drift closed. The next thing she knew, she could smell antiseptic, and the lights were very bright.

"Doc!" he bellowed.

Ahead, a pretty blonde in a white lab coat glanced up. When she spotted Chrissy, relief flashed in her bright-blue eyes.

"Set her down here." Doc Emerson patted an empty bunk. Levi did as ordered, but stayed close, his hand resting on Chrissy's arm.

The doc pulled a scanner over and then lifted a light, shining it in Chrissy's eyes, making her wince.

"It is so good to see you, Chrissy."

Chrissy reached for Levi's hand and felt pain radiate from her fingers to her wrists. He set it back on the bed. "All in one piece, you mean?"

Her attempt at a joke pulled a strangled noise from

Levi, and his fingers tightened on her arm.

Doc Emerson's lips twitched and she lowered her scanner. "You have a minor concussion, and some third-degree burns. All in all, you're a lucky lady." The woman reached over, and lifted a huge syringe filled with silver liquid. "But I'm afraid I still need to give you a shot of nanomeds."

"That's happening to me a lot lately."

"Don't worry, they'll heal you up in no time," the doc assured her.

"I'm sorry for the hassle." Chrissy looked up at Levi. "I'm sorry."

"Quiet." He squeezed her arm.

Looking into his whiskey-brown eyes, she barely even felt the needle as the doc injected the dose of tiny medical machines.

"I need you to rest up here for a bit," Emerson said, wrapping Chrissy's hands loosely with bandages. "I'll be monitoring the nanomeds, and once I think you're stable enough, you can go." She patted the blanket and then moved to a nearby office.

"I'm sorry for what happened at the pool," Chrissy murmured.

Levi blew out a breath and sat on the edge of her bed. "I was an ass. The words you used...they were the same ones my dad used to yell at me when when I was young."

Chrissy sucked in a breath. So that's what had triggered him.

"Every day, he'd tell me that I was useless and worthless, and that he always had better things to do. Which usually included drinking and fucking."

She awkwardly patted his hand with her bandaged one. "I'm sorry."

"Nothing to be sorry for. Life sucks, and you move on."

She frowned at his matter-of-fact statement. There was always some glimmer of good in the bad, but Levi sounded like he always expected the worst.

"My mom died having my little sister." Chrissy fiddled with the sheet. "My dad raised us, but he had no clue what to do with two little girls. I did everything I could to help. Cooked, cleaned, fixed up the messes my wild child sister left behind, became a mechanic like him so I could help in the garage."

"Chrissy—"

"It was never enough. He always complained, or just never noticed." She caught Levi's gaze. "He rarely complimented my work."

Levi cupped her cheek. "And you still grew into a beautiful, sexy, talented, and sassy woman."

Warmth coiled through her. "And you became a relentless force of nature, despite your deadbeat dad."

A smile quirked his lips.

She shook her head. "Well, we sure are a pair, aren't we?"

His thumb brushed her lips. "Yeah."

The infirmary doors opened, and Holmes strode in with Niko and Noah. Chrissy straightened, tugging on the tangled mess of her hair.

"Chrissy." Holmes touched her shoulder. "We are very pleased to see you're okay."

"Thanks."

"Can you tell us what happened?"

She nodded. "One of the alien trike parts I was examining heated up and exploded."

Noah frowned. "They'd all been scanned and deemed inert."

"Well, it fucking wasn't," Levi bit out.

She patted his hand. "We probably need to implement some extra procedures as we continue to work out how to operate the trike."

"We can't afford any delays," Niko said quietly.

"But we can't risk blowing up the Enclave either," Noah said. "I'll have my team work on it with the Hunter mechanics."

"As soon as the doc clears me, I'll get back to work," Chrissy said.

"Hell, no," Levi growled.

She narrowed her gaze. "You don't get to boss me around, biker man."

"I sure as hell do. You want me to tell them what sexy little noises you make when you come?"

She hissed in a breath. "You asshole. You won't be hearing them again."

There was a choked noise and she looked up to see the usually staid general trying very hard not to laugh. Niko and Noah were smiling. Heat burned through her cheeks.

"I think what Levi was trying to say, was that you need some rest," Niko said diplomatically.

"No, what he was trying to do was stamp his claim all over me like a caveman."

Fingers gripped her chin and forced her to look at

him. "You almost died. For twenty agonizing minutes, I thought you were dead."

Her anger crumpled. She saw the agony in his eyes. "Levi."

"Our cue to leave," Noah said.

She didn't watch them go, instead lifting her lips up for Levi's kiss. He kept it gentle and she'd never had gentle from him before.

It wasn't long before Emerson was back. She unwrapped the bandages to expose new, pink skin on Chrissy's hands and feet. She flexed her fingers and toes, relieved there was no pain.

"Well, I think you can go, but I need you to take it easy." The doc moved to probe the almost-healed bump at the back of Chrissy's head. She made a satisfied, humming noise.

"Already?" Levi asked. "You don't want to keep her in here for more observation?"

Emerson lifted a comp pad. "I'll be monitoring the residual nanomeds from here. She's almost healed, so everything should be fine. But if anything does go wrong, you bring her back. For now, she needs someone to take care of her, check on her, and ensure she gets some rest."

Suddenly, Chrissy froze as a thought hit her. "I have nowhere to go. My room—"

All her things were gone. Pain pierced her chest. Her belongings might have been meager, but they'd been *hers*. They'd meant the world to her. Her heart clenched.

"Yes, you do." Levi picked her up, holding her against his chest. "You're coming with me."

Emerson grinned at them. "Good. Macho alpha

males come in handy on occasion. You need someone to look after you, Chrissy, and Levi appears determined to do it..." All of a sudden, Emerson's voice broke off, and her face turned pale.

"Doc?" Levi asked with a frown.

The woman pressed a hand to the bed, and waved with her other one. "I'm...fine." She took a few deep breaths. "As long as the apple I just ate doesn't make a reappearance."

Chrissy cocked her head. She remembered that same look on her sister's face. "You're pregnant."

Emerson gave them a wan smile. "I just found out today. Uh, keep it to yourself, please. I haven't had a chance to tell Gabe yet."

Levi grinned. "The man is going to freak out."

The doctor winced. "Probably."

"Congratulations," Chrissy said.

"Thanks." Then Emerson's face went from white to green. "Ah, I'll see you later." With a flap of her lab coat, she was running for the bathroom.

For a second, Chrissy tried to imagine big, scary soldier Gabe Jackson from Hell Squad as a father. The image just wouldn't appear. The man was beyond intimidating, but she had seen him with Emerson, and it was clear he was both protective as hell and madly in love.

"Come on, Spitfire." Tightening his hold on her, Levi headed out of the infirmary.

"Where are we going?" She should probably see someone about getting new quarters assigned.

"You're coming home with me."

CHAPTER FOURTEEN

L evi carried Chrissy to his room. Once inside, he
took her straight into the bathroom, and set her
down on the closed toilet. She still looked a little shell-
shocked and her face was marred with black ash.

He went to the rarely-used tub and set the water
running. Methodically, he stripped her bare, and then
nudged her into the water.

"Levi—"

"Just let me take care of you." He tipped her head
back, pouring water over her hair. It smelled of smoke
and he wanted her clean.

He didn't have any fancy shampoos or soaps, but he
grabbed his plain shampoo and massaged it into her hair.
He kind of liked the idea of her smelling of his soap. Her
eyes closed, and she made a small moan.

After he'd worked the shampoo through her hair, he
nudged her down into the water to rinse it off. Her hands
gripped the side of the tub. He saw that they were

perfectly healed, the new skin a little pink. But in his head, he kept seeing them blistered and blackened.

His jaw tightened. Images of her room peppered him. The wall blown apart, the space just an empty, black shell. And he remembered the agony of thinking she was dead.

She shifted in the bath, water sloshing against the tiles. She was alive. He stared at the rise and fall of her chest. And he was going to take care of her.

Levi cleared his tight throat. "I'm going to order you some food."

"I'm not very hungry—"

"You'll eat."

Eyes still closed, a small smile tilted her lips. "Bossy biker man."

"Don't you forget it."

Back in the main room, Levi took a minute to order some food from the kitchen. Then he paced, waiting for it to be delivered. He kept trying to block the horror of finding her exploded room. His hands curled into fists. *Fucking Gizzida.* He was laying the blame for this on those damn raptors. Next time he was on a mission, he had some extra anger to work off.

There was a knock at the door, and Levi opened it to a teen boy, who handed over a tray. Levi thanked the kid before slamming the door shut.

He'd just set the tray down on the table when he heard the sobs from the bathroom.

Jaw tight, he walked inside, and saw Chrissy hunched over in the bath, crying.

"Chrissy—"

She looked up, her eyes red. "Those alien parts are destroyed. That could mean that damn trike won't work." A hiccupping breath. "That could ruin the entire mission."

"I don't give a fuck about the trike. You'll figure something out."

She swiped at her eyes. "I barely had any personal things...but now they're gone."

The heartbreak in her face told him this was about more than losing some clothes and things. Without thinking, he toed off his boots, and without stopping to shed his clothes, he climbed into the tub behind her.

She gasped. "Levi."

"Shh." He leaned back against the edge and settled her between his legs. "You're alive, Chrissy. And I'm fucking glad."

A sob broke from her chest. "I didn't think anyone would really care if I died. When I was with the aliens, I knew there was no one out there thinking about me."

He wrapped his arms securely around her, pressing his lips to the side of her head. "Well, not anymore, Spitfire. I care. And there's a young boy here at the Enclave who cares. And I know you're friends with Taylor. She'd care."

Chrissy started crying, turning into him.

Levi had always hated when women cried. Whenever the tears started, he usually got out fast. When his ex had cried, they'd usually been a form of manipulation.

But this time, he didn't feel the urge to run, or fill the space with meaningless words. He held Chrissy until the tears subsided, and then he helped her out of the now-cool bath. He stripped his soaked clothes off and wrapped a towel around his waist. Then he grabbed another towel and started rubbing her down.

"I never had much," he said. "Growing up, my dad was a lazy drunk who only cared about himself."

"I'm sorry," she murmured.

Levi ushered her into the room and straight into his bed. He climbed in beside her, wrapping his arms around her.

"My dad did his best," Chrissy said. "But two girls left him baffled most of the time. He never got over losing my mother." Her gaze flicked up to him. "What about your mom?"

Levi shrugged. "She ran off when I was a kid. She didn't much like having a mean drunk as her old man. Especially when he knocked her around."

"So she left you?" Chrissy's voice rose, revealing a glimmer of his spitfire. "She *left* you with him?"

Levi nodded, amused at the fierce glint in her eye. "Not everyone is like you. I know you saved a kid who wasn't even your own. I guess my mother didn't want to be saddled with a kid. I grew up rough, but I had Ash. And when I was old enough, I learned to fight for what I wanted. Eventually, I took over the Iron Kings and cleaned it up. I was proud as hell of the bikes and cars we put together." Even now, he still felt the bittersweet hit of the loss.

Sweet curves moved against him and Levi fought to remind himself she'd been injured.

"I read about some of your custom builds once. There was an online interview. It was amazing work."

He smiled down at her, but then the pleasure faded. "I lost it all in the invasion. And I lost the men I considered brothers."

A hand cupped his face. "Stuff doesn't really matter, does it? People do."

He nodded. "That's right. And I've got Ash and my squad." He tightened his hold on her. "We go out there and wade into the raptor muck every day. It's not pretty, and there's no beauty, but I always know that they have my back."

They were silent for a while. An easy silence. Levi couldn't remember ever being in bed with a woman like this. He was either fucking or sleeping...not cuddling.

"Tell me more about your dad," he said.

"Typical macho man. He wanted boys. He was a hell of a mechanic, and I followed in his footsteps."

"He should have been proud."

Chrissy snorted. "He was pretty old-school, and thought that I should be married with babies, not swinging a wrench in his workshop." She sighed. "My sister was a wild child. I think it was her way of dealing with the loss of our mom. I always guessed that Jussy felt guilty knowing that mom died from having her. I also have a niece." Chrissy's voice hitched. "They disappeared before the invasion, and I had no idea where they were. I have no idea if they're even alive."

Levi knew that not knowing was sometimes harder than dealing with death. "You're alive, Chrissy." He leaned down, peppering slow kisses across her face. "I really like that you're alive. I like the way you look, the way you smell, the way you throw sass at me."

Her eyes were on his face. "I do not throw sass."

"Woman, you have enough attitude for three women." He caught her hand as she swung at him. "You're also good at your work. Cool as ice in the field, and you swing a wrench like a pro."

She giggled. "I only aimed for your head once."

"The way we strike sparks off each other, I doubt it will be the only time." He kissed her now, slow and deep. He slid his tongue into her mouth, tangling with hers. She lifted a leg, wrapping it around him.

"I should let you sleep," he growled.

"I'm fine," she said huskily.

He was too selfish not to have her. He *needed* to be inside her. "I want to watch your face this time," he murmured. "I want to watch everything on your face when I'm inside you, when you come."

They moved together, and he pulled her towel away. Pushing her back, he cupped her breasts, tugging on her nipples.

She sighed, moving restlessly.

When he slid his hand between her legs, she was already damp and ready for him. "All mine." He lifted his fingers and licked. "And so sweet. So much sweet hidden under the attitude."

"Levi." She writhed on the sheets.

He nudged her legs apart and then he was pushing inside her. "Want to take it slower this time." Except her tight heat was already making desire churn inside him.

Her back arched, her gaze never leaving his. "I just want you."

He started moving, thrusting inside that tight body he

couldn't get enough of. Their gazes stayed locked, and he watched every flicker of pleasure cross her face.

As he moved faster, pumping inside her, she didn't hold anything back. And when she came, crying out his name, he'd never seen anything as beautiful.

With a groan, Levi came, pulsing inside his woman's warmth.

Still catching his breath, he wrapped himself around her. He pressed his fingers to her throat, right over her beating pulse. Alive, sexy, and his.

He listened to the sound of her breathing even out, and not long after, he followed her off to sleep.

CHRISSY SAT inside the alien vehicle, staring at the console. She'd been forced to improvise and put in some Hunter parts, and a few unique printed parts she'd had Bec make for her. She fingered some of the controls, watching her scanner screen.

It wasn't perfect, but it was operational.

She looked out of the vehicle at the small crowd of berserkers standing around the trike. One of her team had added a protective tint to the trike's windshield. She could see out but no one could see in. They didn't want a raptor peering in and seeing humans.

She focused on the berserkers. Damn, they were a wild, handsome bunch. There was enough testosterone right here to power a small city.

She opened her door and climbed out. "It's ready."

She licked her lips, her gaze moving to Levi. To her very own wild berserker. "But..."

"But...?" Levi scowled.

"I'll need to come with you on the mission."

As she'd guessed would happen, he tensed. Since he'd run down that corridor to get to her after the explosion, he hadn't let her out of his sight. The last two nights, they'd slept tangled with each other all night, and she'd woken with him pressed behind her, a hard cock nudging inside her. He'd shadowed her all day as she'd worked to get the trike functional.

"I'm still the best at driving it, but I could teach someone else. The problem is if something goes wrong. I had to cobble things together, splice in some of our parts... and if something goes wrong, which it likely will, you'll need me."

Levi was shaking his head, his hands on his hips, staring hard at the floor.

"We need to get into that dome and see what the aliens are doing." Tane's dark gaze flicked to Levi before landing back on Chrissy.

Damn, the man really had a handsome face, but the intensity of his eyes was enough to make a girl want to hide.

Finally, Tane nodded. "Chrissy's coming with us. Everyone suit up. It's time to go and see what the aliens are hiding. We leave in an hour."

As the others headed off, Levi grabbed her, pinning her up against the trike. He stayed silent.

She watched him, concerned. She couldn't get a read

on him. "This is where you explode and tell me that it's too dangerous."

"Where I tell you it fucking terrifies me to take you into that dome." His forehead dropped against hers. "But I know you're right. I know we need you."

Her chest swelled. "Levi—"

"And I know I'll keep you safe. You're mine to protect now."

"Is that right?" She felt a flood of emotion take up residence in her chest.

"Yep. Your sexy mouth is mine, your fantastic hair is mine, your gorgeous breasts, your tight, wet—"

"I get the picture," she said dryly.

He kissed her. "Let's go get ready."

"I need to go and see Max, first," she said. "Explain where I'm going."

He nodded. "I wish we had time to go back to our room and—"

She pressed a finger to his lips. "When we get back, biker man. I'll meet you back here in an hour."

Chrissy hurried down to Max's quarters and spent a few minutes with the boy, explaining that she was going back out on a mission. Thankfully, he didn't quite grasp the danger, and was more excited that she was going to spend time with the berserkers. She ruffled his hair and gave him a tight hug. She couldn't tell him that there was a chance she might not make it back.

Back in her borrowed armor, her laser pistol and her tools strapped to her hips, Chrissy walked back to the Hunter hangar.

"Chrissy!" Taylor jogged up to her. "I heard about the mission."

Chrissy nodded. "Thought a trip to the ocean might be nice."

Taylor smiled, but her gaze was serious. "Be careful out there. I know your berserker will take care of you, but come home safely."

Chrissy hugged her friend. "Will do."

In the Hunter hangar, a small crowd was gathered around the alien vehicle.

The berserkers were all there, weapons slung over broad shoulders. Hemi was clearly telling a joke, and the others were smiling. But she felt the tense readiness pumping off them.

General Holmes and Niko stood nearby.

Holmes nodded to her. "Good luck, Chrissy. Thank you for doing this."

She nodded and moved over to join Levi and the others.

"Levi, you ride up front with Chrissy," Tane said. "The rest of us will be in the back."

Chrissy blew out a breath and climbed into the vehicle. Levi waited until the others were in the back before he settled into the seat beside her.

Now or never. She fired up the engine, and tested the controls. Swallowing her nerves, she set them in motion and soon they were heading up the ramp to the surface.

"Slow and steady, babe," Levi said as they headed out into the sunlight. "My favorite way to fuck you."

"Levi!"

"Actually, I like hard and fast too, and sweet and sexy. Frankly, any time I'm inside you is my favorite."

"I'm on the line here, Levi," came Indy's dust-dry voice through the comms.

Chrissy felt heat flare in her cheeks.

"Cool it," Indy continued, "Or I'll have to go and take a cold shower."

"You need a man, Indy," Levi said.

A snort. "Men are trouble."

"She's not wrong," Chrissy muttered.

Levi grinned, and soon they turned off the Enclave road onto one of the main roads. The sun was setting, drenching everything in golden light. She pulled the controls, turning the trike to head north, toward Sydney. It would be dark by the time they reached the city.

Her hands flexed on the controls. "We might not make it back."

"That's always a risk." Levi reached over and gripped her hand. "But Squad Three is damn good at what we do. Berserkers never give up. We keep fighting."

She smiled. "You just like blowing things up."

He winked at her. "That, too."

The drive was tense. Chrissy kept expecting to be confronted by aliens—more trikes or maybe one of the giant rexes the raptors saddled and rode. She scanned the sky for any sign of raptor ptero ships. The muscles in her arms and shoulders wound tighter and tighter. Thankfully, the alien vehicle performed well, and her patch jobs held.

"Chrissy, pull to a stop near the three-story building on the right," Indy said. "You have an alien convoy incoming. I suggest you let them pass, and then pull in behind to join them."

Chrissy pulled the trike to a stop and waited. She tapped her foot on the floor, her pulse pounding as she stared out at the shadowed street.

"Hold it together, Spitfire."

"What if they confront us?" she said. "Or one of these parts fail, and they come to help us?"

"And what if we drive right into that dome undetected and get what we need?"

She closed her eyes, trying to relax. "You're right." She opened them and saw the line of alien trikes appear, their headlights spearing into the night. They lumbered down the road in single file. She watched them pass, one by one.

"Go," Indy said. "And good luck."

Chrissy pushed the controls and they rolled forward. She turned the vehicle, falling in behind the last trike.

"And remember," Indy said, "once you're in the water and inside the dome, I won't have contact with you."

They'd be on their own.

Chrissy followed the convoy, waiting for one of the other vehicles to drive back and demand to know who they were. But the convoy rolled on, headed toward the Sydney Airport.

They were getting closer to the ocean. They turned a corner and ahead, Chrissy got her first look at the hulking shadow of the alien mothership parked on the old runways of the airport. She gasped.

Levi reached out again, patting her thigh. "First time you see it, it packs a punch."

She nodded, speechless. It was lit up with lights that glowed white and red. It looked like some giant, crouching creature, poised to dive into the waters of Botany Bay.

Then the alien convoy turned again. They skirted the airport, and the submerged wreckage of the port appeared directly ahead.

The lead alien vehicle drove into the water and disappeared.

Chrissy took a deep breath. It would be their turn soon.

One by one, the other alien trikes drove down the ramp and into the water.

Hands shaking, Chrissy drove them forward, and they made their descent. Water lapped at the hood, then the windows, and then they were fully submerged.

It was darker than she'd imagined. Ahead, their lights illuminated the back of the alien trike ahead of them. She followed, gripping the controls tightly. *Don't drive off the edge. Don't drive off the edge.*

The ramp evened out, the path leading directly to the orange dome appearing ahead.

God, it was incredible and terrifying. And it was far bigger than it had appeared in the spiderbot footage.

She watched as the alien vehicles ahead of them drove inside the dome through a huge, gate-like entrance.

"Here we go," Levi murmured.

Then it was their turn.

Body tense, Chrissy drove them through the arch. This close, she could see the orange substance of the dome was covered in small black striations, almost like veins.

They entered some sort of vestibule. A second later, there was a whoosh of sound as the water rushed out. Then, a second door ahead opened automatically.

Chrissy set the trike moving and they drove into the alien dome.

CHAPTER FIFTEEN

L eaning forward, Levi stared out through the windshield. *Fuck.*

Alien vehicles were all over the place, as well as giant gantry cranes overhead. Armed raptors were everywhere.

Ahead, a huge, lumbering alien that he'd never seen before was making its way across the dome. It was at least four times the size of the raptors, and its arms were so long, its knuckles almost dragged on the ground. Most raptors had scaly skin in shades of gray. This one's skin was green. It made Levi think of an ogre. And damn, there were two more of the things in the dome.

He watched as one of the big creatures lifted up some huge boxes and carried them across to the other side of the dome.

As the ogre moved away, Levi got a glimpse of the center of the dome.

What the hell? His gaze narrowed. A giant, black octagon about the size of a truck rested in the very middle of the dome. Raptors were moving around it, working on it.

"What the hell is that?" Chrissy asked.

"I don't know." He pulled out a small recording device and started snapping pictures. He knew that as soon as they got out, Tane would set loose a small mini-drone that would scan the octagon and gather data. It would be stored in Tane's helmet cam.

Regardless, whatever the hell that thing was, it wasn't going to be good.

"A weapon?" Chrissy suggested. "A bomb?"

"Probably." It was certainly something the Gizzida didn't want them to see. His gut tightened. Something designed to stamp out the last of the human survivors.

"Indy?" Levi waited a beat, but as expected, there was no response. "Tane?"

"We're here." Tane's deep voice came through loud and clear. "Can't see anything from back here. What's happening?"

"We're in the dome. Raptors everywhere. There's a giant octagon device in the center of the dome. Looks like some sort of weapon."

"Record it." Tane's voice was grim. "As soon as I can, I'll set the mini-drone free."

"I'm going to do a lap of the dome," Chrissy said, following some of the vehicles. "See if I can get us closer to the device."

Levi studied her. She was tense, but holding it together. Fucking gorgeous and brave. No way in hell he was letting her go.

"Uh-oh," she said.

"What?"

She pointed. He peered out and saw that raptor soldiers were waving the row of vehicles into a parking zone not too far ahead.

And another team of raptors was opening the back of each vehicle and pulling gear out.

"Shit. Let's take that path over there." Away from the raptors.

She nodded, turning their trike away from the others. A raptor stepped forward, waving his arms at them. She ignored him and drove on.

Levi heard shouts and saw that raptor break into a jog. "He's not very happy with us."

"They aren't going to just let us go," Chrissy said, her voice tense.

He looked out the side window, and saw several raptors jogging after them, their scaled weapons clutched in their hands. *Fuck.*

Suddenly, a giant scaled foot slammed down in front of them. Chrissy made a strangled sound, and dodged it, tires screeching. The ogre shifted, and this time, a giant fist crashed into the ground ahead of them.

Chrissy swerved, the back end of the trike sliding out. They skidded into some stacks of equipment and boxes flew everywhere. The trike came to a shuddering stop, rocking on its wheels.

"What the hell is going on!" Tane's taut voice.

"A fucking problem. They're onto us. Tane, we're going to have to fight our way out."

"That's what we're good at," his leader replied.

"Levi." Chrissy's eyes were wide.

He reached over and yanked her in for a hard kiss. "I'm getting us out of here. There are still lots of naughty, dirty things I want to do to your body."

A shocked laugh escaped her. "You're thinking about sex at a time like this?"

He stroked her cheek. "I'm always thinking about sex when I'm around you."

"Don't get hurt," she ordered.

Levi looked out the windshield and saw a group of raptors charging at them. He twisted his neck to loosen it, letting the fury that drove him ignite.

He looked back at his woman. "I *will* get you out of here." He opened the door, seeing the rest of his squad leaping out of the back of the vehicle. "Stay back here and hide. I'll be back for you."

Then he lifted his carbine and turned to fight.

TERROR WAS an ugly hole in Chrissy's gut. She ducked down, but kept peeking out the window, trying to keep Levi and the other berserkers in view.

As the soldiers charged forward, she saw Tane pause and lift his palm into the air. She couldn't see it, but she knew he must have set the mini-drone free.

Mission accomplished. Now they just had to get out of here and get the intel back to the Enclave.

God, there were aliens everywhere.

She watched the berserkers move together, carbines up and firing. They were a breathtaking sight. She watched them charge into the oncoming raptors, and heard their wild cries as they clashed with the enemy.

No hesitation. They were tough, protective, and ferocious.

The squad broke off, fighting in pairs. She watched Levi and Ash fighting together, taking down two raptors with hard blows and wild carbine fire.

Suddenly, a hail of raptor poison sprayed toward the squad. They all ducked and rolled, taking cover behind the parked trikes and stacks of alien gear.

Her throat tightened. There were so many raptors. How the hell were they ever going to get out of here? Six men, no matter how fierce and tough, weren't going to be able to fight off an army of aliens alone.

She saw Levi leap up. An alien raptor swung at him and he ducked, then slammed a hard punch into the alien's gut. He followed it with an unforgiving front kick. The raptor stumbled back with a roar and Levi stepped over him, carbine aimed down.

Ash jumped off some crates, spraying laser fire everywhere. The berserkers mowed through raptor after raptor. God, was Hemi actually laughing?

They were so good, but crazy.

Movement caught her gaze and she saw one of the giant knuckle-dragger creatures lumber closer. Her blood turned to ice. The damn thing was huge and powerful. It lifted its foot and slammed it down near the berserkers.

She saw Tane shouting and waving an arm. Her hands pressed to the armor on her thighs. Griff was fighting off two raptors and the giant alien was headed after him.

All of a sudden, Levi leaped out, waving his arms at the alien.

Her heart lodged in her throat. God, he was drawing its attention.

The creature swung around, its large, red eyes zeroing in on Levi. It stomped in his direction. The creature lifted its foot again and brought it down with a *boom*. It landed close to Levi. Too close. He rolled to get out of the way.

Chrissy couldn't breathe. She watched the monster fixing its crimson gaze on Levi, lifting its foot again.

Levi rolled again, hitting some crates. Several toppled over, and one crashed down on his leg.

The knuckle-dragger let out a deafening roar and moved toward Levi.

"Get up, biker man." Mouth dry, she watched him grimace, trying desperately to free his leg.

Wildly, she looked around, expecting Ash to be charging in to help his friend. But Ash was wrestling with a raptor. And the other berserkers were fighting their own battles. They were too far away.

Screw this. Sick of watching and feeling helpless, she started the trike's engine. Her hands clenched on the controls.

The alien lifted its foot, aiming directly at Levi.

She accelerated fast, the trike shooting forward. She saw Levi's head snap up. She aimed right at the alien's other leg.

She dodged some boxes and picked up more speed.

Chrissy rammed into the alien.

The impact was bone-crunching, and she was tossed forward. She looked up and saw the creature teetering.

Fall. Fall. It hung there for a second, swaying slightly back and forth, and started to plummet backwards. Chrissy grinned...until the creature kicked out its leg.

Its huge foot slammed into her vehicle.

The world upended, and she rolled over and over. Chrissy squeezed her eyes shut and ducked her head. Glass smashed with a hard crackle, and she felt a sharp sting on her face, followed by a hard knock to her shoulder.

The trike came to a stop on its roof. Pain throbbed through her and she opened her eyes.

The windshield was completely destroyed, and from what she could see of the trike, it was dented and twisted.

She pulled in a shaky breath. But she was alive, and she was pretty sure nothing was broken. Was Levi okay?

The door was wrenched open with a screech of metal.

Smiling, she looked up, expecting to see Levi.

Dread filled her, and her heart thumped in her chest.

A raptor leaned down and grabbed her armor at the back of her neck. With a grunt, he dragged her out of the vehicle.

CHAPTER SIXTEEN

L evi sprayed carbine fire at more incoming raptors. *He had to get Chrissy.*

"Plan B!" Tane shouted.

Plan B was to blow stuff up and make a mess. They were all carrying small charges with a localized blast radius. The theory being that they could blow shit up and not bring the entire dome and ocean down on their heads.

But right now, Levi didn't give a fuck about the mission. Chrissy had blazed past like some damn warrior woman and crashed the trike into the damn ogre. *Shit. Be okay, Spitfire.*

A raptor got close and Levi kicked him, spun under the alien's swinging arm and jabbed an elbow into the raptor's chest. Some close-range fire of the carbine, and the enemy was down.

"Ash!"

His best friend spun, face lined with sweat. "I got to get to Chrissy."

Ash nodded. "Got your back, bro."

"And Ash? I go down, you promise me you'll get her out."

Ash's eyes flashed. "You aren't fucking going down."

"Promise me."

"Fuck yeah, I'll get her out," Ash ground out.

Levi nodded. Ash would never let him down. More raptors charged forward with a thunder of boots. Alien poison sprayed, and Levi ducked it. He crouched down behind some crates. Then he darted out, keeping low, and heading closer to the crashed trike.

Out of the corner of his eye, he spotted Ash steadily fighting his way closer to him.

Another ogre roared from nearby. Levi spun and looked up. The creature was batting at its chest. Levi squinted and spotted Dom scaling the creature, ramming his knives into the beast to help him upward.

Fuck. Levi watched Dom climb up onto the ogre's shoulder, ignoring its clumsy swings. Then he leaped into the air and rammed his blade into one of the alien's eyes.

The creature staggered backward, letting out a pained cry. It started to topple over...

Dom leaped off and hit the ground with a graceful roll. A second later, the ogre's head exploded.

Levi kept moving, ducking and weaving through crates and equipment. Most of it was black or made of bone, and some of it blinked with red lights. Finally, he caught a glimpse of the trike. His hands clenched on his carbine. The vehicle was battered to hell, and resting on its roof.

Then his blood ran cold. A raptor was dragging a struggling Chrissy out of the vehicle.

Levi fought the instinctive need to instantly charge in. The bastard raptor shook her, and Levi caught a glimpse of her terrified face. He knew that she already had so many bad memories, and this had to be bringing them back.

Fuck this.

He jumped up, moving forward and firing. Several raptors shouted, running in his direction.

Come on, assholes. Viciously, he took down another raptor and crashed past a second one.

"Levi, wait!" Tane shouted.

"I have to get to Chrissy."

"*Wait.* We're right behind you."

Levi knew his squad was coming. Behind him, he heard several muted booms from their explosives. He paused, and saw the raptor shake Chrissy again. Then the alien lifted his weapon, pointing it at her head.

Fear, slick and oily, oozed in his gut. "No!"

Levi charged forward. He couldn't wait for his squad. He'd almost lost her once already, and there was no way in hell he was letting her die here.

The raptor spun, its demonic red gaze narrowing on him. The alien shifted his weapon, taking aim at Levi. Levi huffed out a sharp breath. Instead of the usual weapon that spat green poison at them, this was a deadly crossbow, filled with wicked, needle-sharp, bone projectiles.

As the raptor fired, Levi leaped onto the top of a

parked trike. He ran across the roof, hearing bone bolts ping off metal. Then he vaulted off it.

"Levi! Stay back," Chrissy screamed.

He felt something hit his chest. He winced, but thankfully the projectile hadn't pierced his armor. Something winged his arm, making his left bicep sting, but he ignored it.

He didn't care. He had to get to his woman.

He was running full pelt now. He heard carbine fire, knew his squad was giving him cover fire. They'd pick off as many raptors as they could. Ash and the berserkers always had his back.

There was another volley of projectiles. He felt a sharp pain in his ribs and he stumbled.

"Levi!" Chrissy's panicked scream.

He didn't stop, bringing his carbine up in one hand, and his laser pistol in the other. Another projectile hit him, this time, tearing through his armor and into his left thigh.

Agony.

His leg went out from under him, and he went down on one knee. He gritted his teeth through the shooting pain and heard Chrissy scream his name.

CHRISSY STRUGGLED against her captor's hard grip, fighting back tears.

Levi was coming for her—charging toward her like some kind of wicked, avenging angel.

She watched him push back up to his feet, wavering slightly before he started forward again.

Coming for her. Fighting for her.

The raptor beside her took aim again.

No way. She rammed into him. "You aren't killing him, asshole!"

The alien turned and backhanded her. The blow lifted her off her feet, and she slammed into the overturned trike before sliding to the ground. Winded, she searched for Levi.

He was still firing and limping forward. His face was set in hard lines, determination radiating off him. She knew he'd never stop. The rough edges and cockiness didn't change what he was—a true hero.

And then she realized something that sucked the last of the air from her lungs. She was falling in love with him.

The raptor stepped forward, raising that deadly weapon again. She *had* to stop him.

Chrissy fumbled on her belt and yanked out the pistol Levi had given her. She lifted it, hands shaking, and aimed.

She pulled the trigger. Her aim was crap, but she still hit him. The raptor jerked and turned. Now, he turned his weapon on her.

"Not today, fucker." Levi leaped onto the raptor's back. They both crashed to the ground. Chrissy scrambled backward, watching them wrestle. Then she pushed to her feet and hurried over. When she had the perfect shot of the raptor's back, she fired.

The alien roared, and tossed Levi off him. Levi

whipped his carbine up and started firing. Chrissy moved in beside him, adding her pistol to the barrage.

Together, the two of them advanced on the raptor. With another roar, the alien fell to his knees, and a second later, he went down.

God. Chrissy spun and threw her arms around Levi. He pulled her close, holding her so tight she couldn't breathe.

"Are you okay?" she asked.

"I am now."

She pulled back and spotted a bone projectile sticking out of his thigh. Bile rose in her mouth. "Oh, God. We need to get that out."

"It'll have to wait for now." He turned, his face turning granite hard. "First priority is getting out of here. *Now.*"

She turned and followed his gaze.

Oh. God.

The berserkers were running at full speed toward them. Explosions detonated behind them, backlighting them with gold flames.

And through the flames, every alien in the dome was mobilizing and moving right behind the squad.

Her stomach dropped. They were trapped in the middle of the alien dome with no way out.

LEVI'S SQUAD MATES ARRIVED, surrounding them.

"We need a way out," Tane growled, looking around. "And we need it now."

Levi looked at the horde of incoming aliens. They needed it yesterday.

"We could steal another vehicle," Chrissy suggested.

"They've barricaded the main door." For once, Hemi's face was serious, their dire circumstances reflected in his dark eyes.

Tane shook his head. "They'd blow us to hell as soon as we got close."

Levi scanned the dome, his jaw tight. He was not letting Chrissy die here, and he hadn't fucking planned to die today, either.

"Holmes said there was only one way in and out," Griff said, his voice gruff. "And we can't reach Indy for more options."

"Setting off the last of our charges," Dom said, holding up a small detonator. He touched a button.

Boom. Boom. Boom.

Boxes and raptors flew into the air. Guttural shouts and screams filled the dome.

Levi looked at Chrissy and saw she was staring upward.

"Look." She pointed up. "Over there."

Levi followed her gaze, scanning the gantry scaffold she was pointing to. A large crane was attached to the side of the dome and surrounded by bone-mesh walkways. There were several ladders leading up.

"What?" he said. "We use the crane to smash a hole through the dome?" They'd all drown before they got out.

She shook her head and pointed again. "The hole."

"Shit," Tane said quietly.

That's when Levi spotted them. Up on the gantry, two water raptors carrying propulsion units in their clawed hands, were reentering the dome through a small, circular opening.

"The drone team missed that," Tane said.

Levi grinned. "We can use the propulsion units to get to the surface."

"And everyone has their breathers," Tane said.

The tiny units clamped into a swimmer's mouth and let them breath for a certain period of time. Levi yanked his off his belt and helped Chrissy do the same.

She grimaced. "What about that giant aquatic alien?"

Yeah, he didn't like knowing that massive carnivore was out there, swimming around. Hell Squad had tangled with it once before, and Shaw had nearly lost his life.

"Let's hope it's sleeping," Levi said.

"We don't have any other options," Tane said grimly. "We'll have to risk it." He looked around, eyeing his men. "Squad Three, let's climb that gantry, and get the hell out of here."

"Time for a swim," Hemi said cheerfully.

They raced toward the nearest ladder.

"Hemi and Griff, we need cover fire," Tane ordered.

Smoothly, both men swiveled and lifted their carbines.

"I have some smoke grenades," Hemi said with a wide grin.

Griff nodded, pulling grenades off his belt. "And I have some frag ones."

"Let's make a mess," Hemi said.

As Tane started up the ladder, Levi urged Chrissy toward the first rungs, and tried to block the pain in his leg. It was as if a hot knife was slicing into him, over and over. He locked his jaw and forced himself to move. He'd make it. No matter what.

Chrissy moved upward, climbing fast. He took a millisecond to appreciate that armor-covered ass. Yep, he was getting her out of here. Then he was finding a bottle of bourbon and keeping her in his bed. For a week.

He started up, blocking the agony. Dom and Ash started up the ladder right behind him. He could hear Griff and Hemi firing, and then the bang hiss of a smoke grenade, followed by the thump of the exploding frag grenade. He looked down, casting one last glance at the strange octagon device.

We'll be back for you.

When he pulled himself onto the platform, Chrissy was crouched nearby. Her gaze was glued on Tane, who was fighting the two water raptors.

"Holy hell," she murmured.

Yeah, Tane was a force of nature. Levi watched the squad leader with a mixture of respect and envy. It was hard, rough, and dirty fighting. Tane's face was lethal and focused, and when he fought, he was all strength and power. With a few more lethal blows, he slammed one raptor headfirst into the metal railing with a *clang*. Then he gripped the second alien, spun, and tossed the raptor off the gantry.

He looked back at them, thoroughly calm. "Come on."

Levi pushed Chrissy ahead. Behind him, Dom and

Ash were giving Hemi and Griff cover fire as they climbed. Some raptors were returning fire and he heard projectiles hitting the platform nearby. He pushed Chrissy ahead of him, shielding her body.

Reaching Tane, they stopped beside a row of the propulsion units stored against the dome wall.

Tane grabbed one and hefted it. "Damn, it's heavy."

As the others joined them, Tane shoved the unit at Griff.

"Two people for each unit. I'll take one myself." He hefted another unit and handed it to Hemi.

When Tane handed one to Levi, he gritted his teeth. It was fucking heavy, and his leg screamed, threatening to fail. But then Chrissy was there, lifting the other side and helping him carry it.

They turned to the black, circular doorway. It was a couple of feet wide, and made of a rubbery substance that they'd have to squeeze through.

Suddenly, a roar echoed around them and one of the ogres slammed a fist into the platform nearby. The structure crumpled and tilted. Levi grabbed onto the railing.

"Go! Go!" Tane yelled.

Griff and Dom shoved their breathers into their mouths, then pushed through the rubbery membrane with the propulsion unit and disappeared.

"Go, Tane," Hemi ground out. "You have the intel."

A muscle ticked in their leader's jaw. "You'd better be right behind me." He turned and pushed through.

"We're up, Spitfire." Levi leaned in and gave her a quick kiss. "Take a deep breath, and remember all those naughty, dirty things I want to do to you when we get home."

Hemi leaned in from behind them. "I want to hear more about these naughty, dirty things."

Chrissy shook her head, elbowing Hemi playfully. Then the ogre roared again and she turned back to face the membrane. "I'm ready."

"Hold on tight to this thing." Levi pressed her hands down to the handholds on the unit. "And remember, I'm with you. All the way."

He moved in behind her, caging her in between himself and the propulsion unit.

Then they both put their breathers in their mouths and pushed through the membrane.

For a second, it felt like being smothered by a latex blanket. Then the water hit Levi's face.

CHAPTER SEVENTEEN

Chrissy's heartbeat echoed loudly in her ears.

She dragged in air through the breather, staring ahead through the pitch-black water. Levi flicked on a light on the propulsion unit and it cut through the darkness. She felt his hands touch something on the unit. It vibrated, and they powered up through the water with a wash of bubbles.

As they moved, fish darted out of their way, and ahead, she saw the shadows of Griff and Dom, and Tane, not too far above them.

But damn, it was so black and suffocating.

Already, she felt a tickle in her lungs. She wanted to wrench the breather from her mouth and take a huge breath. Instead, she focused on Levi. His protective arms were tight around her, and she moved one hand to grip his wrist.

A flash of movement to her left made her turn her head. She saw nothing but black. When she turned back, she bumped against Levi and the breather fell from her mouth.

No! She almost lifted a hand off the propulsion unit, but fought the urge. Levi hadn't noticed and she didn't want to worry him. She focused on holding her breath.

But it wasn't long before her lungs started to burn.

Don't open your mouth. Don't open your mouth. God, she couldn't hold her breath much longer.

How much farther? She looked up, but couldn't tell if the surface was getting closer.

Then, something sliced through the water to her right, and she turned her head. Without any goggles, her vision was blurry, but in the gloomy light from the unit, she caught a clear glimpse of a giant shadow cutting through the water.

It was bigger than any shark she'd ever seen.

Oh, God. Primal fear clamped down at the base of her neck. She felt Levi tense, and knew he'd seen it, too.

Chrissy kept searching the water. *Where the hell was it?* She prayed the damn thing wasn't behind them. She caught another glimpse of it to their left, huge flippers carving through the water. This time, it was close enough that she saw a giant mouth filled with rows of sharp, wicked teeth. It disappeared with a flick of a solid, forked tail.

She felt sick. Jeez, one damn killer alien after another.

She kept turning her head, fighting the need to open her mouth. Her chest was in agony, and her head felt like it was stuck in a clamp. Her lungs were at the breaking point. She couldn't keep her mouth closed any longer...

They broke the surface. Chrissy gasped, heaving in air.

"You okay?" Levi's hand was on her back, rubbing. "We made it."

She nodded, wiping water off her face. "Did you see it?" She turned her head, scanning the surface.

It was dark and choppy, and they bobbed up and down with the waves. They were right at the entrance to the bay and she could see the lights from the airport in the distance. Moonlight gleamed from overhead.

Levi's face hardened. "I saw it."

"What do we do?" She looked back toward the shore. It looked *so* far away. God, that *thing* could be right under them. She tried not to hear that threatening *da-dum, da-dum* tune in her head, but it started, mocking her.

"Well, let's hope it isn't hungry," Levi said dryly.

Chrissy splashed water at him. "Be serious."

Seconds later, the other berserkers moved over to join them, and Ash and Hemi broke the surface.

"We have a problem," Ash said.

"A big one," Hemi added. "A fucking big, killer aquatic monster. It knows we're here, and it's interested."

Just as Hemi finished talking, the creature broke surface. They all spun, treading water, and watched the gray hump of the alien creature's back breach the surface. All the men moved, raising their carbines.

The aquatic alien dived and disappeared back below the waves.

Suddenly, a *boom*, followed by another, shattered the quiet. Chrissy turned again and looked toward the airport. Smoke was rising into the air. Another explosion blasted into the night sky in a ball of flames and smoke.

"What's going on?" Griff said.

"Must be our guys," Tane said. "We have no comms, so I don't know for sure."

"Keeping the alien reinforcements off us, maybe?" Hemi suggested.

The aquatic alien surfaced again, circling closer. This time, Ash and Levi opened fire. The creature thrashed, setting them all bobbing in the wild waves.

Chrissy gripped Levi's arm. She kicked her legs faster to keep her head above the surface.

"Head to the shore," Tane ordered. "The southern side of the bay, away from the airport."

Chrissy's gut cramped and Levi aimed the propulsion unit toward land. She tightened her hold and they zoomed forward. But she was pretty sure that they'd never make it. It was too far, and the creature in the water could move faster. It would take them all down before they even got close to land.

"Chrissy, you go ahead." Levi moved to let go of the unit.

She shook her head, grabbing his hand. "And leave you to get eaten alive to save me? No!" She tightened her hold

"Stubborn woman. I said *go*."

"When have I ever followed your orders, biker man?"

"When I've had you naked."

She hissed out a frustrated breath. "Well, I'm not naked now."

His jaw clenched. "I won't let you die."

"Guys," Ash snapped.

Chrissy saw the ripple in the distance and her chest tightened. The aquatic alien was powering through the water, coming straight at them.

They were out of time.

"Go!" Tane yelled.

Levi kept a tight hold on Chrissy's hand as he jerked the unit around and set them off again. Water hit her face as they raced toward the shore.

"By the way, I love you," she yelled.

Levi looked over at her, shocked. "What?"

"I thought you should know."

"Fuck," Levi shouted back. "I love you too, Spitfire."

From nearby, Ash laughed. "You owe me two month's clothing credits, Rahia."

Hemi chuckled. "Thought he'd hold out a bit longer."

Behind them, the creature reared out of the water, cutting off the banter.

"Faster!" Tane roared.

But there was no way they'd be fast enough. Despair choking her, Chrissy looked back and watched the huge jaws open. It was almost on them.

She gripped Levi's hand hard. "Levi."

"Look at me, Spitfire. Only me."

She looked into those whiskey eyes...and suddenly laser fire erupted behind them.

Chrissy choked on a scream. The water churned as the alien creature's huge body jerked and lurched, shuddering under the impact of the weapons fire.

A dark, metallic smell filled the air as the alien's

blood spilled into the water, and she looked up to see two Hawks materialize above them.

One quadcopter swung around, still firing on the beast, green laser lighting up the night. The creature was no longer moving, and it slowly sank beneath the waves.

Shocked at the suddenness of the attack, Chrissy just stared. The other Hawk lowered down directly above them, its skids only a meter off the water. The side door slid open.

Claudia and Marcus from Hell Squad were there, holding out hands to them.

"Need a ride?" Claudia asked.

Elation burst inside Chrissy and all she could do was nod. The rest of Hell Squad stood behind the pair in the Hawk, carbines in hand.

"Hell yeah, we need a ride." Levi boosted Chrissy upward.

Claudia gripped her hand and pulled her inside the Hawk.

"Hey, that's our saying," Shaw called out from his spot on the cannon nearby. He had the weapon aimed at the water.

Marcus leaned down and helped Levi aboard. As her man hugged her tightly to him, Chrissy watched Hell Squad help the rest of the berserkers into the quadcopter.

"Let's roll, Finn," Marcus ordered, slamming the door closed.

The Hawk turned on the spot and then flew south-west.

"What's happening at the airport?" Tane asked, shaking the water out of his hair.

"We heard the alien chatter go haywire, and knew you guys were in trouble," Marcus said. "We knew we'd need some firepower to help you, especially since you were right under the noses of the largest concentration of fucking aliens in the area."

Tane tilted his head. "But you couldn't bring all the squads and risk leaving the Enclave defenseless."

Marcus nodded. "Squad Nine's on the other Hawk, and the general couldn't authorize sending another squad. But, we also needed to keep the fuckload of aliens at the airport busy."

"Who?" Tane asked.

"Manu demanded Holmes send him and a team of volunteers in."

Chrissy watched Tane's face change. It was microscopic, but she thought she saw both worry and pride.

Hemi dropped into a seat, leaning back. "If anyone can make a mess and keep the aliens scrambling, it's Manu."

Levi sat in a seat and tugged Chrissy onto his uninjured thigh.

"Your wound?" She tried to get up.

"Hold still. Need to hold you."

She stilled instantly. "Will Manu be okay?" She knew the former soldier had a prosthetic leg.

Levi nodded. "Toughest man I know. When he lost his leg...it was brutal, but the tough bastard kept fighting all the way back to the Hawk. He'll be more than okay. He'll make the Gizzida wish they'd picked a different fucking planet to invade."

Chrissy relaxed against Levi, her taut body finally

realizing they were safe. She sent up a little prayer for Manu, and whoever was with him. Then she breathed in the scent of the man she was in love with, and who was in love with her.

They were alive and safe, and for now, that was enough for her.

Manu

MANU FINISHED SETTING the last batch of charges under some stacked crates. Swiveling, he jogged back toward the pickup point, trusting his armor's illusion system and the darkness to keep him hidden from the nearby raptors.

He pushed for more speed. He was almost as fast as he'd been before his prosthetic leg. It was state-of-the-art, stolen by Hemi and Tane when they'd snuck into the city to find it for him. They'd been more upset when he'd lost his leg than he had.

Manu had trained hard on the treadmill to adjust to his different balance, and it had paid off. He lengthened his stride, enjoying being outside.

He lifted his head and saw the Gizzida mothership looming above.

Okay, maybe he wasn't enjoying being outside as much as he could. Anger—sharp and visceral—cut through his gut.

These motherfuckers had come here to tried and destroy. Manu had no idea if his family—his beloved mother—in New Zealand had made it. The Rahia clan had been sprawling and close, and he knew in his heart that not all of them would have made it.

And the bastards had taken his leg. He might have adjusted to life without it, but that didn't mean he couldn't lay the blame where it was deserved.

The Gizzida had thought Earth was going to be an easy target. Manu smiled grimly. They'd been wrong.

Ahead, he saw a sagging wire fence and a row of warehouses beyond it.

"Incoming," he murmured.

"We see you," the cool female voice in his earpiece replied.

He wondered if that voice ever heated. Did she get angry? Did that voice turn husky when she was turned on?

Not now, Manu.

He quickly scaled the fence, cursing when his prosthetic foot slipped. He paused, adjusted, and kept moving. He dropped down on the other side and ran.

His practiced eye spotted the shimmer that he knew was the camouflaged Hawk. They'd taken a huge fucking risk parking themselves practically on top of the alien mothership, but they'd had no choice.

As he approached, the side door slid open. He saw Captain Kate Scott waving him aboard.

Manu took two steps and jumped. He landed inside the Hawk, wincing when he felt a pain flare up his thigh, where his prosthetic was attached.

Kate slammed the door closed. "Let's go."

Manu nodded his thanks, and then turned to the rest

of his makeshift team. "Jacob, you ready to set those charges off?"

The young man nodded. "Yes, sir."

Damn, the boy made Manu feel old. With a small lurch, the Hawk lifted off.

"Then do it," Manu ordered.

The man lifted his small detonator and thumbed the control. The first explosion made the Hawk rock as they rose higher in the air. Manu leaned against the side door, looking out the small window. Below, he saw the explosion had the raptors scrambling.

A second explosion followed, moments later.

"Bring us around," Manu called out to the pilot.

The Hawk wheeled around to the left.

Below, the ground rumbled and flared with more explosions, but Manu knew there weren't many left. It wasn't enough.

He palmed the specially modified grenades clipped to his belt. They were his own creations. Running the firing range at the Enclave kept him busy, but he always had time on his hands to play. Especially with things that made aliens go boom.

He pulled the door open, the wind rushing into his face.

"What are you doing?" Kate called out.

He lifted a grenade. "Making more of a mess." He activated the explosive and tossed it over the side.

Manu watched it fall until it was out of sight. *One. Two. Three. Four.*

Boom.

"Wow." A young female soldier leaned in from behind Manu. "Those things pack a punch."

"Sure do. Maddy, fly closer to the mothership."

The female pilot yelled back, "On it, Manu."

God, he'd missed this. He thought about his brothers, out there risking their lives. He hoped to hell they were okay, and that he could buy them enough time.

"Berserkers are tough."

Kate's voice made him glance up. She wasn't even looking at him, but she'd clearly read his mood. She was sitting on the cannon beside him, her hands light on the controls.

"They'll make it," she said, matter-of-factly. "So, let's keep these aliens busy so your brothers can get away."

Hell, yeah. Manu yanked more grenades off his belt, handing one to the soldier hovering behind him. The woman's eyes lit up as she took it.

They dropped several more and were doing another pass, when projectiles peppered the side of the Hawk.

Fuck. Manu ducked back, cursing under his breath. "Shit, can they see us?"

Kate shook her head. "They're guessing from the trajectory of the bombs. Sniper."

Manu had one more grenade in his hand. He leaned out again and tossed it.

More bone-like projectiles slammed into the Hawk. Kate swiveled her cannon, her face intent. "I see him."

She opened fire. Manu watched the laser arc through the sky seconds before a small building below went up in rubble and flames. He saw the body of a raptor get tossed into the air. Smoke billowed upward. Hell, she was good.

"You got him!" Manu turned his head, looking into cool, blue eyes. "Nice shooting."

She gave one short nod.

"Oh, God, surface-to-air missiles incoming!" Maddy's panicked shout from the cockpit. "Everyone hold on!"

The young pilot threw the Hawk into evasive maneuvers. Manu grabbed the side of the door, holding tight. He needed to get the door closed. He reached for the latch, but a second later, the Hawk jerked wildly.

"One rotor's hit!" Kate yelled.

The Hawk shuddered, tilting to the side.

Manu lost his grip, sliding toward the open door.

Shit. He reached out, trying to grab onto something to stop his slide.

Suddenly, a body slammed into him, knocking him in the opposite direction and back into the Hawk. They hit the floor, Manu on the bottom and Kate on top.

The Hawk leveled out.

"Jacob, get that door closed," Kate ordered.

"Yes, Captain."

Kate looked down at Manu. "Are you all right?"

"I am. Thanks to you."

"Don't mention it." Her hands flexed on his chest, like she was about to push off him. Her gaze dropped down, skating down his body.

Manu was suddenly aware of the compact, curvy body under her fatigues. Strong legs were straddling his hips. Manu was a big man, and he'd always liked strength in a woman.

Her gaze lifted and met his. For the briefest second, he saw a flash of heat in the blue before she hid it.

She quickly climbed off him. "Maddy, report?"

"We're okay," the pilot called back. "We can make it back to base. And I just got an update from the Enclave. Squad Three made it! They're on their way back."

Manu sat up, releasing a breath. *Thank God.*

His gaze drifted back to the oh-so-capable Captain Scott. That small glimpse of heat had intrigued him.

He'd noticed her before. She was about his age, fit and athletic, and spent a lot of time in the firing range. But she was serious, worked a lot, and kept to herself. She was contained. Usually, Manu had always been attracted to outgoing women with a healthy sense of humor.

But something about the composed captain got to him. And he'd always been a man who liked getting to the bottom of things.

"Let's go home," he called out. "We've all earned the right to get back and celebrate."

The volunteers cheered, and the captain studiously avoided looking at him.

CHAPTER EIGHTEEN

"Harder, Spitfire. Take more."

As Chrissy slid up and down on Levi's cock, he groaned. She was riding him hard and it was heaven.

He was sitting in a chair in his quarters, Chrissy's naked breasts bobbing in front of his face as she moved. He felt his orgasm rushing closer, his balls tightening.

"I'm close," she panted, her hands digging into his shoulders.

Levi closed his mouth on one of her breasts. She moaned his name, sliding down and taking him deep.

God, she was perfect. He slid one hand between her thighs and stroked. "Fuck, you feel so good stretched around my cock, Chrissy."

"Yes." She moved against him.

He thumbed her clit, rubbing hard.

"Oh...*Levi*." She threw her head back. "I love you."

And a second later she was coming, her body clamping down on his cock and milking him hard.

He wrapped his arms around her and slammed her down. "Love you, too."

With his cock deep inside her, he came hard, shouting her name.

She collapsed against him, her face pressed to his neck. *Damn*. Levi wasn't sure he could feel his toes. He stroked her back.

"Next, I'm going to suck your cock in the shower," she murmured.

He groaned, sliding a hand into her hair. He tilted her head back, studying her face. "Babe."

"Don't 'babe' me."

It wasn't that he didn't appreciate the non-stop sex and orgasms. They'd been at it for hours since they'd returned from the mission and Levi had been patched up in the infirmary. But he knew his woman well enough now to know that there was something else driving her.

"We're alive, Chrissy. We made it."

Her eyelids fluttered before she looked away. "We almost didn't make it." She shuddered, and he knew she was thinking of the raptors pulling her out of the trike, and that damn water monster.

He stroked her cheek. "But we *did*. I know you feel the need to prove it. To know that we're both breathing, and believe me, I love the way you're going about it—"

She rewarded him with a feminine snort.

"But since I just came inside you three times, I'm going to need an hour or two to gather my strength for the next round."

She smiled, leaning in to kiss him. It was a slow, sexy kiss. Levi let her take the lead, savoring the taste of her. He'd never kissed or been kissed like this before.

Finally, she lifted her head. "Well, we do have a party to get to, anyway."

He nodded. He knew that Niko had organized a party to try and lift the morale of the Enclave. Word of the mysterious black octagon was out, and speculation was rife. Everyone was tense and worried. "I could do with a drink."

She pressed a hand over his heart. "Thanks for coming for me, in the alien dome. You just charged forward, like a warrior, and I've never had anyone love me that much."

Fuck, she undid him. "I will always come for you. Besides, you helped, Chrissy. It wasn't me crashing trikes into giant alien ogres and finding a way out of the dome. Without you, the mission would've gone south." He slid both hands into her glorious auburn hair. "We're alive. I need you to remember that shit happens, will always happen, but we keep getting back up, and life goes on."

She nodded. "I lost everything. I came here with nothing. My father's dead, and I don't even know if my sister and niece are alive. Now I have something I never expected—" she pulled in a deep breath. "I don't want to lose you too, Levi."

"I know. I'll do my best to make sure that doesn't happen. I've never had beauty like you in my life, and this time, I'm keeping it. And, babe, I'm a berserker, remember? We're tough."

"And wild and crazy," she added, stroking his goatee.

"Life goes on, and you and I are going to suck the marrow out of it." He slid a hand down to cup her breast before he slid it lower and spread his palm over her belly. "One day—not yet, but one day—I want to see this round with the baby I planted in it."

Her breath hitched. "Caveman."

"Yep." He smiled at her. "Hey, I just remembered that I have something for you."

Her eyes lit up. "Really?"

"Don't sound so surprised." He set her on her feet and walked to a nearby shelf. He held out a small package wrapped in hand-painted paper.

She turned it over, then tore it open like a kid on Christmas. She held up the two candles, her eyes going wide. "You...got me candles."

"Taylor told me you liked them."

"My biker man got me candles."

Jeez, she looked like he'd beaned her over the head with her own wrench.

She sniffed one and then the other. Warmth filled her eyes. "Vanilla and mango. My favorites."

He shrugged, uncomfortable now. "It's no big deal."

"It is to me, biker man." She leaned in and kissed him. A second later, the candles thudded on the floor and he yanked her up on her toes, deepening the kiss.

"Shit, maybe I should let you suck my cock in the shower."

She pushed against him. "Too late now. I want to go to the party."

"Damn." He reached over and gave her a quick slap on the ass. "Then you'd better go and put on something pretty, babe. Something that I'll want to tear off you later."

Naked, she sauntered to the closet. "Don't 'babe' me."

CHRISSY FINGERED the fabric of the pretty green dress she was wearing. It had a deep *V*-neckline and was short.

Levi had surprised her with some clothes when they'd returned from the mission. Since hers were all charcoal, it had really touched her. And he'd given her candles.

Her man could be thoughtful...and damn, he must really love her.

Holding Levi's hand, she walked with him into the Garden. She breathed deep, savoring the lush scent of blooming flowers. From the first moment she'd arrived at the Enclave, this had become a favorite place to visit. It was a bowl cut into the rock at the top of an escarpment above the Enclave. The residents reached it through a tunnel, and the Garden had a retractable roof that opened up to let the sunshine in. At all times, it was hidden by an illusion system. Here, the Enclave's residents could walk on the grass, and enjoy the greenery and sunshine. Off to the side were rows of garden beds where they grew fresh fruits and vegetables.

This evening, people stood around eating, laughing, and drinking. Kids were playing, running through the trees, and by the picnic tables, she saw off-duty squad soldiers enjoying their downtime.

She and Levi joined the berserkers, who were sharing beers with Hell Squad. Tane was standing, nursing a beer. Hemi was sprawled in a chair, with Cam in his lap. Griff, Dom, and Manu were talking quietly with Shaw and Claudia, and Reed and his fiancée, Natalya. Ash had Marin tucked in front of him, and she was talking animatedly with Elle, who was standing with one hand tucked in the back pocket of Marcus' jeans.

Ash eyed them both, a smile on his face. It was easy for Chrissy to tell that Ash was happy that his best friend had fallen in love. Levi and Ash started talking.

She shifted her head to glance at Tane, who looked deep in thought and was staring into the trees. She followed his gaze, and saw he was watching Selena. The alien woman was so pale she was almost glowing. She was walking barefoot through the grass, smiling. Her long platinum hair fell around her shoulders and she wore a simple green dress that accented her startling green eyes.

"She's pretty," Chrissy murmured.

Tane didn't shift his gaze. "Look at her feet."

Chrissy did and gasped. With each step, flowers bloomed to life under Selena's small feet.

Now Tane looked at Chrissy, an unreadable look on his face. "She's powerful, and I don't think anyone here realizes just how much."

Swallowing, Chrissy watched Selena disappear into the Garden. The woman was their ally, and an enemy of the Gizzida. Chrissy had heard rumors of the woman's affinity to nature and her abilities. Which included saving Marin's life.

Tane set his drink down and followed Selena into the trees.

"Chrissy, I hear you let this wild berserker catch you," an accented voice drawled.

She turned back and saw Cruz smiling at her. He was standing with a tiny baby resting on his shoulder, and her tiny, diapered bottom cupped in one of his big palms. There was no sign of his wife, Santha, so Chrissy assumed the woman was working. God, watching Cruz hold the baby with such ease made her ovaries want to explode. Especially after what her bad-boy biker had said to her back in their room.

"You heard wrong." She shot Levi a saucy look. "I caught him."

Everyone laughed, and Levi gripped the back of her neck and squeezed. Hearing children's voices and laughter, she turned her head and spotted Max. He was running with some friends. When he spied her, he grinned, and gave her a big wave. She waved back, so happy to see him carefree. His lost family and his time with the aliens would never be forgotten, but life did go on. He was happy, and his scars were fading.

"The tech team have any luck working out what this octagon device is?" she heard Levi ask Marcus.

Marcus shook his head. "They're still analyzing the pics and scans you guys brought back. Nothing yet." The rugged man scowled. "I spent last night without my wife in my bed. She was glued to her comp in the lab."

Elle smiled. "Actually, Gaz'da is helping us and its speeding things up a lot."

Chrissy leaned into Levi, darkness trying to creep into the happy feeling. She wasn't entirely sure how she felt about the raptor-turned-ally that lived at the Enclave. He stayed out of sight, and was helping them, but her months of captivity meant she had trouble accepting him. She thought of that damn octagon device instead.

"I hate not knowing."

"We know more than we did before," Levi said. "Whatever the hell that thing is, we keep fighting, no matter what they throw at us."

She smiled. She knew her man would never give up.

"There's always hope, Spitfire." He winked. "Plus, I'm always ready for a fight."

She shook her head and chuckled.

Suddenly, Gabe Jackson stormed into the group. The big man reached over and snatched Cruz's drink out of his hand and knocked it back.

Chrissy raised her brows and glanced sideways to see Levi grinning.

Gabe dropped onto one of the picnic table chairs, and it creaked under his muscular form. He reached for Shaw's drink, but the sniper snatched it back.

"No way," Shaw said.

Reed handed his cup over, and Gabe took it and drank it in one gulp.

"Gabe." Marcus rested his hand on the man's shoulder.

Hell Squad's deadliest soldier looked up, his normally dark face pale.

"I think I know what this is about," Chrissy said.

Levi lifted his glass. "Congrats, man."

"What's going on?" Claudia demanded with a frown.

Gabe opened his mouth, then closed it. When he stayed silent, Chrissy cleared her throat. "Emerson's pregnant."

"What?" A smile broke out on Claudia's face.

A round of cheers and laughter broke out.

"Awesome, man." Shaw clapped Gabe on the back.

Cruz jiggled baby Kari. "It's the hardest job in the world." The baby gurgled at her father, and his handsome face softened. "And it's the best damn job in the world."

"She's pregnant with twins," Gabe ground out.

There were gasps.

Claudia was trying hard not to laugh. "I thought twins came from the mother's side?"

"I don't know," Gabe said. "What the hell do I know about babies?"

"Gabe," Marcus said. "You're a good man, an excellent soldier, and you'd die for your woman." Marcus lifted his beer and sipped. "You'll be fine. And Doc Emerson will help you work it out. Together."

The tiniest bit of color came back into Gabe's rough-hewn face.

"We need drinks," Shaw called out.

When Levi slid his arm across Chrissy shoulders, she smiled. Life did go on. And in the squads and family units in the Enclave, there was goodness to celebrate. There was love worth fighting for. Nothing was shiny and perfect anymore, and it didn't matter. It stripped everything back to what was really important.

She felt a rough hand tease the skin on her thigh, just under the hem of her dress.

"Want to get out of here?" Levi murmured. "I suddenly feel the need to get you naked again."

Desire spiked. "I could be talked into it."

"You're fucking perfect." He pressed his lips to hers. "And all mine."

"Yes, I am."

"I told you I always get what I want."

She shook her head. "Cocky and arrogant."

"Yep."

"Let's sneak out." She grabbed his hand, pulling him toward the door.

But they'd barely taken two steps when strong arms circled her waist and she was lifted off her feet. She found herself tossed over Levi's shoulder.

As he strode through the crowd, she heard laughter, cheers, and whistles.

"This isn't sneaking, biker man!"

"Don't care." He slapped her butt. "You're all mine, Spitfire, and I want the world to know that."

Chrissy didn't mind the world knowing it, but she still put up a fight. There was no way she'd let her man get his own way without a little pushback. She needed to keep him in line.

But deep inside, her heart now belonged to her cocky, arrogant biker man and she wouldn't have it any other way.

I hope you enjoyed Levi and Chrissy's story!

Hell Squad continues with MANU, starring former berserker and oldest Rahia brother, Manu. Coming in 2018.

For more action-packed romance, read on for a preview of the first chapter of *Gladiator,* the first book in my best-winning Galactic Gladiators series.

Don't miss out! For updates about new releases, action romance info, free books, and other fun stuff, sign up for my VIP mailing list and get your *free box set* containing three action-packed romances.

Visit here to get started: www.annahackettbooks.com

FREE BOX SET DOWNLOAD

JOIN THE ACTION-PACKED ADVENTURE!

PREVIEW: GLADIATOR

MORE SCI-FI ROMANCE

Fighting for love, honor, and freedom on the galaxy's lawless outer rim.

Fighting for love, honor, and freedom on the galaxy's lawless outer rim...

When Earth space marine Harper Adams finds herself abducted by alien slavers off a space station, her life turns into a battle for survival. Dumped into an arena on a desert planet on the outer rim, she finds herself face to face with a big, tattooed alien gladiator...the champion of the Kor Magna Arena.

A former prince abandoned to the arena as a teen, Raiden Tiago has long ago earned his freedom. Now he rules the arena, but he doesn't fight for the glory, but instead for his own dark purpose—revenge against the Thraxian aliens who destroyed his planet. Then his existence is rocked by one small, fierce female fighter from an unknown planet called Earth.

Harper is determined to find a way home, but when she spots her best friend in the arena—a slave of the evil Thraxian aliens—she'll do anything to save her friend... even join forces with the tough, alpha male who sets her body on fire. But as Harper and Raiden step foot onto the blood-soaked sands of the arena, Harper worries that Raiden has his own dangerous agenda...

Just another day at the office.

Harper Adams pulled herself along the outside of the space station module. She could hear her quiet breathing inside her spacesuit, and she easily pulled her weightless body along the slick, white surface of the module. She stopped to check a security panel, ensuring all the systems were running smoothly.

Check. Same as it had been yesterday, and the day before that. But Harper never ever let herself forget that they were six hundred million kilometers away from Earth. That meant they were dependent only on themselves. She tapped some buttons on the security panel before closing the reinforced plastic cover. She liked to dot all her *I*s and cross all her *T*s. She never left anything to chance.

She grabbed the handholds and started pulling herself up over the cylindrical pod to check the panels on the other side. Glancing back behind herself, she caught a beautiful view of the planet below.

Harper stopped and made herself take it all in. The orange, white, and cream bands of Jupiter could take your breath away. Today, she could even see the famous super-storm of the Great Red Spot. She'd been on the Fortuna Research Station for almost eighteen months. That meant, despite the amazing view, she really didn't see it anymore.

She turned her head and looked down the length of the space station. At the end was the giant circular donut that housed the main living quarters and offices. The main ring rotated to provide artificial gravity for the residents. Lying off the center of the ring was the long cylinder of the research facility, and off that cylinder were several modules that housed various scientific labs and storage. At the far end of the station was the docking area for the supply ships that came from Earth every few months.

"Lieutenant Adams? Have you finished those checks?"

Harper heard the calm voice of her fellow space marine and boss, Captain Samantha Santos, through the comm system in her helmet.

"Almost done," Harper answered.

"Take a good look at the botany module. The computer's showing some strange energy spikes, but the scientists in there said everything looks fine. Must be a system malfunction."

Which meant the geek squad engineers were going to have to come in and do some maintenance. "On it."

Harper swung her body around, and went feet-first down the other side of the module. She knew the rest of the security team—all made up of United Nations Space Marines—would be running similar checks on the other modules across the station. They had a great team to ensure the safety of the hundreds of scientists aboard the station. There was also a dedicated team of engineers that kept the guts of the station running.

She passed a large, solid window into the module, and could see various scientists floating around benches filled with all kinds of plants. They all wore matching gray jumpsuits accented with bright-blue at the collars, that indicated science team. There was a vast mix of scientists and disciplines aboard—biologists, botanists, chemists, astronomers, physicists, medical experts, and the list went on. All of them were conducting experiments, and some were searching for alien life beyond the edge of the solar system. It seemed like every other week, more probes were being sent out to hunt for radio signals or collect samples.

Since humans had perfected large solar sails as a way to safely and quickly propel spacecraft, getting around the solar system had become a lot easier. With radiation pressure exerted by sunlight onto the mirrored sails, they could travel from Earth to Fortuna Station orbiting Jupiter in just a few months. And many of the scientists aboard the station were looking beyond the solar system, planning manned expeditions farther and farther away. Harper wasn't sure they were quite ready for that.

She quickly checked the adjacent control panel. Among all the green lights, she spotted one that was blinking red, and she frowned. They definitely had a problem with the locking system on the exterior door at the end of the module. She activated the small propulsion pack on her spacesuit, and circled around the module. She slowed down as she passed the large, round exterior door at the end of the cylindrical module.

It was all locked into place and looked secure.

As she moved back to the module, she grabbed a handhold and then tapped the small tablet attached to the forearm of her suit. She keyed in a request for maintenance to come and check it.

She looked up and realized she was right near another window. Through the reinforced glass, a pretty, curvy blonde woman looked up and spotted Harper. She smiled and waved. Harper couldn't help but smile and lifted her gloved hand in greeting.

Dr. Regan Forrest was a botanist and a few years younger than Harper. The young woman was so open and friendly, and had befriended Harper from her first day on the station. Harper had never had a lot of friends —mainly because she'd been too busy raising her younger sister and working. She'd never had time for girly nights out or gossip.

But Regan was friendly, smart, and had the heart of a steamroller under her pretty exterior. Harper always had trouble saying no to her. Maybe the woman reminded her a little of Brianna. At the thought of her sister, something twisted painfully in Harper's chest.

Regan floated over to the window and held up a small tablet. She'd typed in some words.

Cards tonight?

Harper had been teaching Regan how to play poker. The woman was terrible at it, and Harper beat her all the time. But Regan never gave up.

Harper nodded and held up two fingers to indicate a couple of hours. She was off-shift shortly, and then she had a sparring match with Regan's cousin, Rory—one of the station engineers—in the gym. Aurora "Call me Rory or I'll hit you" Fraser had been trained in mixed martial arts, and Harper found the female engineer a hell of a sparring partner. Rory was teaching Harper some martial arts moves and Harper was showing the woman some basic sword moves. Since she was little, Harper had been a keen fencer.

Regan grinned back and nodded. Then the woman's wide smile disappeared. She spun around, and through the glass Harper could see the other scientists all looking around, concerned. One scientist was spinning around, green plants floating in the air around him, along with fat droplets of water and some other green fluid. He'd clearly screwed up and let his experiment get free.

"Lieutenant Adams?" The captain's voice came through her helmet again. "Harper?"

There was a sense of urgency that made Harper's belly tighten. "Go ahead, Captain."

"We have an alarm sounding in the botany module. The computer says there is a risk of decompression."

Dammit. "I just checked the security panels. The

locking mechanism on the exterior door is showing red. I did a visual inspection and it's closed up tight."

"Okay, we talked with the scientist in charge. Looks like one of her team let something loose in there. It isn't dangerous, but it must be messing with the alarm sensors. System's locked them all in there." She made an annoyed sound. "Idiots will have to stay there until engineering can get down there and free them."

Harper studied the room through the glass again. Some of the green liquid had floated over to another bench that contained various frothing cylinders on it. A second later, the cylinders shattered, their contents bubbling upward.

The scientists all moved to the back exit of the module, banging on the locked door. *Damn.* They were trapped.

Harper met Regan's gaze. Her friend's face was pale, and wisps of her blonde hair had escaped her ponytail, floating around her face.

"Captain," Harper said. "Something's wrong. The experiments have overflowed their containment." She could see the scientists were all coughing.

"Engineering is on the way," the captain said.

Harper pushed herself off, flying over the surface of the module. She reached the control panel and saw that several other lights had turned red. They needed to get this under control and they needed to do it now.

"Harper!" The captain's panicked voice. "Decompression in progress!"

What the hell? The module jerked beneath Harper.

She looked up and saw the exterior door blow off, flying away from the station.

Her heart stopped. That meant all the scientists were exposed to the vacuum of space.

Fuck. Harper pushed off again, sending herself flying toward the end of the module. She put her arms by her sides to help increase her speed. Through the window, she saw that most of the scientists had grabbed on to whatever they could hold on to. A few were pulling emergency breathers over their heads.

She reached the end of the pod and saw the damage. There was torn metal where the door had been ripped off. Inside the door, she knew there would be a temporary repair kit containing a sheet of high-tech nano fabric that could be stretched across the opening to reestablish pressure. But it needed to be put in place manually. Harper reached for the latch to release the repair kit.

Suddenly, a slim body shot out of the pod, her arms and legs kicking. Her mouth was wide open in a silent scream.

Regan. Harper didn't let herself think. She turned, pushed off and fired her propulsion system, arrowing after her friend.

"Security Team to the botany module," she yelled through her comm system. "Security Team to botany module. We have decompression. One scientist has been expelled. I'm going after her. I need someone that can help calm the others and get the module sealed again."

"Acknowledged, Lieutenant," Captain Santos answered. "I'm on my way."

Harper focused on reaching Regan. She was gaining

on her. She saw that the woman had lost consciousness. She also knew that Regan had only a couple of minutes to survive out here. Harper let her training take over. She tapped the propulsion system controls, trying for more speed, as she maneuvered her way toward Regan.

As she got close, Harper reached out and wrapped her arm around the scientist. "I've got you."

Harper turned, at the same time clipping a safety line to the loops on Regan's jumpsuit. Then, she touched the controls and propelled them straight back towards the module. She kept her friend pulled tightly toward her chest. *Hold on, Regan.*

She was so still. It reminded Harper of holding Brianna's dead body in her arms. Harper's jaw tightened. She wouldn't let Regan die out here. The woman had dreamed of working in space, and worked her entire career to get here, even defying her family. Harper wasn't going to fail her.

As the module got closer, she saw that the security team had arrived. She saw the captain's long, muscled body as she and another man put up the nano fabric.

"Incoming. Keep the door open."

"Can't keep it open much longer, Adams," the captain replied. "Make it snappy."

Harper adjusted her course, and, a second later, she shot through the door with Regan in her arms. Behind her, the captain and another huge security marine, Lieutenant Blaine Strong, pulled the stretchy fabric across the opening.

"Decompression contained," the computer intoned.

Harper released a breath. On the panel beside the

door, she saw the lights turning green. The nano fabric wouldn't hold forever, but it would do until they got everyone out of here, and then got a maintenance team in here to fix the door.

"Oxygen levels at required levels," the computer said again.

"Good work, Lieutenant." Captain Sam Santos floated over. She was a tall woman with a strong face and brown hair she kept pulled back in a tight ponytail. She had curves she kept ruthlessly toned, and golden skin she always said was thanks to her Puerto Rican heritage.

"Thanks, Captain." Harper ripped her helmet off and looked down at Regan.

Her blonde hair was a wild tangle, her face was pale and marked by what everyone who worked in space called space hickeys—bruises caused by the skin's small blood vessels bursting when exposed to the vacuum of space. *Please be okay.*

"Here." Blaine appeared, holding a portable breather. The big man was an excellent marine. He was about six foot five with broad shoulders that stretched his spacesuit to the limit. She knew he was a few inches over the height limit for space operations, but he was a damn good marine, which must have gone in his favor. He had dark skin thanks to his African-American father and his handsome face made him popular with the station's single ladies, but mostly he worked and hung out with the other marines.

"Thanks." Harper slipped the clear mask over Regan's mouth.

"Nice work out there." Blaine patted her shoulder.

"She's alive because of you."

Suddenly, Regan jerked, pulling in a hard breath.

"You're okay." Harper gripped Regan's shoulder. "Take it easy."

Regan looked around the module, dazed and panicky. Harper watched as Regan caught sight of the fabric stretched across the end of the module, and all the plants floating around inside.

"God," Regan said with a raspy gasp, her breath fogging up the dome of the breather. She shook her head, her gaze moving to Harper. "Thanks, Harper."

"Any time." Harper squeezed her friend's shoulder. "It's what I'm here for."

Regan managed a wan smile. "No, it's just you. You didn't have to fly out into space to rescue me. I'm grateful."

"Come on. We need to get you to the infirmary so they can check you out. Maybe put some cream on your hickeys."

"Hickeys?" Regan touched her face and groaned. "Oh, no. I'm going to get a ribbing."

"And you didn't even get them the pleasurable way."

A faint blush touched Regan's cheeks. "That's right. If I had, at least the ribbing would have been worth it."

With a relieved laugh, Harper looked over at her captain. "I'm going to get Regan to the infirmary."

The other woman nodded. "Good. We'll meet you back at the Security Center."

With a nod, Harper pushed off, keeping one arm around Regan, and they floated into the main part of the science facility. Soon, they moved through the entrance into the central hub of the space station. As the artificial gravity hit, Harper's boots thudded onto the floor. Beside her, Regan almost collapsed.

Harper took most of the woman's weight and helped her down the corridor. They pushed into the infirmary.

A gray-haired, barrel-chested man rushed over. "Decided to take an unscheduled spacewalk, Dr. Forrest?"

Regan smiled weakly. "Yes. Without a spacesuit."

The doctor made a tsking sound and then took her from Harper. "We'll get her all patched up."

Harper nodded. "I'll come and check on you later."

Regan grabbed her hand. "We have a blackjack game scheduled. I'm planning to win back all those chocolates you won off me."

Harper snorted. "You can try." It was good to see some life back in Regan's blue eyes.

As Harper strode out into the corridor, she ran a hand through her dark hair, tension slowly melting out of her shoulders. She really needed a beer. She tilted her neck one way and then the other, hearing the bones pop.

Just another day at the office. The image of Regan drifting away from the space station burst in her head. Harper released a breath. She was okay. Regan was safe and alive. That was all that mattered.

With a shake of her head, Harper headed toward the Security Center. She needed to debrief with the captain and clock off. Then she could get out of her spacesuit and take the one-minute shower that they were all allotted.

That was the one thing she missed about Earth. Long, hot showers.

And swimming. She'd been a swimmer all her life and there were days she missed slicing through the water.

She walked along a long corridor, meeting a few people—mainly scientists. She reached a spot where there was a long bank of windows that afforded a lovely view of Jupiter, and space beyond it.

Stingy showers and unscheduled spacewalks aside, Harper had zero regrets about coming out into space. There'd been nothing left for her on Earth, and to her surprise, she'd made friends here on Fortuna.

As she stared out into the black, mesmerized by the twinkle of stars, she caught a small flash of light in the distance. She paused, frowning. What the hell was that?

She stared hard at the spot where she'd seen the flash. Nothing there but the pretty sprinkle of stars. Harper shook her head. Fatigue was playing tricks on her. It had to have just been a weird trick of the lights reflecting off the glass.

Pushing the strange sighting away, she continued on to the Security Center.

Galactic Gladiators

Gladiator

Warrior

Hero

Protector

Champion

Barbarian

Rogue

Also Available as Audiobooks!

PREVIEW: AMONG GALACTIC RUINS

MORE ACTION ROMANCE?

ACTION
ADVENTURE
TREASURE HUNTS
SEXY SCI-FI ROMANCE

When astro-archeologist and museum curator Dr. Lexa Carter discovers a secret map to a lost old Earth treasure—a priceless Fabergé egg—she's excited at the prospect of a treasure hunt to the dangerous desert planet of Zerzura. What she's not so happy about is being saddled with a bodyguard—the museum's mysterious new head of security, Damon Malik.

After many dangerous years as a galactic spy, Damon

Malik just wanted a quiet job where no one tried to kill him. Instead of easy work in a museum full of artifacts, he finds himself on a backwater planet babysitting the most infuriating woman he's ever met.

She thinks he's arrogant. He thinks she's a trouble-magnet. But among the desert sands and ruins, adventure led by a young, brash treasure hunter named Dathan Phoenix, takes a deadly turn. As it becomes clear that someone doesn't want them to find the treasure, Lexa and Damon will have to trust each other just to survive.

The Phoenix Adventures

Among Galactic Ruins
At Star's End
In the Devil's Nebula
On a Rogue Planet
Beneath a Trojan Moon
Beyond Galaxy's Edge
On a Cyborg Planet
Return to Dark Earth
On a Barbarian World
Lost in Barbarian Space
Through Uncharted Space
Crashed on an Ice World

Cruz

Gabe

Reed

Roth

Noah

Shaw

Holmes

Niko

Finn

Theron

Hemi

Ash

Also Available as Audiobooks!

The Anomaly Series

Time Thief

Mind Raider

Soul Stealer

Salvation

Anomaly Series Box Set

The Phoenix Adventures

Among Galactic Ruins

At Star's End

In the Devil's Nebula

On a Rogue Planet

Beneath a Trojan Moon

Beyond Galaxy's Edge

On a Cyborg Planet

Return to Dark Earth

On a Barbarian World

Lost in Barbarian Space

Through Uncharted Space

Crashed on an Ice World

Perma Series
Winter Fusion

A Galactic Holiday

Warriors of the Wind
Tempest

Storm & Seduction

Fury & Darkness

Standalone Titles
Savage Dragon

Hunter's Surrender

One Night with the Wolf

For more information visit AnnaHackettBooks.com

ABOUT THE AUTHOR

I'm a USA Today bestselling author and I'm passionate about **_action romance_**. I love stories that combine the thrill of falling in love with the excitement of action, danger and adventure. I'm a sucker for that moment when the team is walking in slow motion, shoulder-to-shoulder heading off into battle. I write about people overcoming unbeatable odds and achieving seemingly impossible goals. I like to believe it's possible for all of us to do the same.

My books are mixture of action, adventure and sexy romance and they're recommended for anyone who enjoys fast-paced stories where the boy wins the girl at the end (or sometimes the girl wins the boy!)

For release dates, action romance info, free books, and other fun stuff, sign up for the latest news here:

Website: www.annahackettbooks.com